The

Greatest Roman

St. Paul

by

Donald Fairburn

Copyright September 21, 2021
Donald Fairburn
All rights reserved

When times of trouble come,
He shall set me high upon a rock
Above my foes, and keep me safe.

Psalm 27: 5 - 6

Subjects

Part I - Luke

1   The Sources: Today
3   Speaking for the Defense: 1,970 years ago
4   A Gentile Physician:
5   A Paralegal Companion:

Part II - Saul

7   A Beginning: 1 AD
11   A Young Boy in Jerusalem: 16 AD
14   A Young Rabbi in Tarsus: 20 AD
15   The World beyond Tarsus: 30 AD
19   A New Calendar: 33 AD
24   Saul's Mission: Late spring, 33 AD
27   Saul Begins His Campaign: Early summer, 33 AD
32   Greater Attention from Saul:
36   Saul's Fury Unleashed: 33 to 36 AD
37   The Entrapment of Stephen:
40   The Stoning of Stephen:
41   Saul's Uncertainty:
43   The Way to Damascus:
45   Saul Begins His Journey of a Lifetime:
47   Saul Reaches Damascus:
49   Medhat Basha:
52   The Rejection of Saul in Damascus:
53   Saul in Jerusalem:
55   Saul is Called to Antioch in Syria: 45 AD
57   Famine and Dispute at Jerusalem: 46 AD
60   Ordination at Antioch: 47 AD

Part III - Paul

61	Saul Becomes Paul:
65	Paphos to Perga: Late June, 47 AD
68	On to Iconium:
71	Iconium and Lystra:
74	Peaceful Derbe:
74	The End of the First Journey: Winter, 48 AD
76	The Impact of the First Journey: Summer, 49 AD
76	A Fundamental Doctrine:
78	The Council at Jerusalem: Autumn, 49 AD
82	The 2nd Missionary Journey of Paul: Fall, 49 AD
83	Map of Paul's 2nd Journey:
86	Across the Aegean to Philippi: Spring, 50 AD
89	The Egnatian Way to Thessalonica:
90	Bound for Beroea:
91	Athens:
94	Corinth:
95	Cenchreae and Homeward:
96	Ephesus, Caesarea, and Jerusalem:
96	Home to Antioch: Late 51 AD

Part IV - The Final Witness

98	Paul's Arrest: Spring, 57 AD
104	The Plot to Assassinate Paul:
106	Paul's Trial before Antonius Felix:
110	Paul's Trial before Porcius Festus:
111	Paul's Trial before Agrippa:
114	Paul Goes to Rome: Fall, 59 AD
120	Safe on the Island of Malta:
123	The End and the Beginning:

Postscript

Preface

This is a story about a man who lived two thousand years ago. It tells about his achievements and his failures; some of the good things he did and a few of the bad things. All of these are found in history books, but please don't expect a history treatise in these pages. I hope to honor the historic facts of his life, but I have taken the liberty to imagine Paul's thoughts while he roamed the streets of Jerusalem as a young rabbinical student; and to guess at his concerns as he rode a clumsy donkey through the mountains of central Turkey. I can even visualize him debating Saint Stephen on Jewish theology, but then I must return to the reality that Paul actually chose to have Stephen stoned to death.

Paul's schooling as a rabbi is told in a fictional setting, but is based upon the facts that we do have on his education and his teacher Gamaliel. And even though there is good reason to believe that he was married, references to his wife are few and only guesswork, since there is no hard data on this aspect of his life.

However, his physician Luke, who treated him as a patient, traveled with him as a missionary, and sailed with him to Rome as a prisoner to be judged by the Emperor Nero, provides enough first hand historical evidence to describe Paul as - -

The Greatest Roman.

PART I - Luke

The Sources: Today

To describe events that happened two thousand years ago is a tedious challenge, but it is also a very rewarding project. Still, care must be taken when those events are of a religious nature, since this may draw a particularly active level of criticism. And if miracles are involved, then the level of scrutiny is enhanced by those who are justifiably skeptical. However, resolving skepticism is far beyond the present task, which is simply to provide my personal depictions of thoughts, words, and exciting adventures that happened many, many years ago.

Those exciting adventures are those of the Apostle Paul, who was born simply as a Roman citizen, but died as the greatest of them all. My intention is to show that Paul's evangelical witness throughout Asia Minor, Greece, and Italy produced a greater benefit to civilization than did any Roman ruler, philosopher, or military commander. Despite the impact made by the Romans on our art, laws, and culture, Paul's impact on the way we live was far greater than that of any other Roman. As Jesus brought God's message to the world, Paul brought the message of Jesus to the Roman Empire.

The Bible is my primary source of data. However, there are other early documents that provide clarification and support to the biblical accounts. These other, non-canonical documents, speak to the cultural and religious conflict that existed throughout the Mediterranean world of two thousand years ago.[1]

The need for these non-canonical documents is further justified by the "book burning" carried out by the Emperor Diocletian from 303 to 311 AD. Those nine years saw the destruction of many Christian documents which, if available, would have made this task much easier and far more informative. However, Diocletian's persecution ironically may have resulted in greater accuracy in copying the manuscripts that had survived, since his persecution made them so rare that they commanded even greater respect and dedication to accurate preservation.

An example of apocryphal data is the *Acts of Barnabas,* reputedly written by the Apostle Mark. This is particularly appropriate, since both Barnabas and Mark accompanied Paul on his first mission trip to Cyprus. Of course, being non-canonical, great care is needed to avoid the very weakness which may have caused a document's exclusion from the cannon in the first place.

In order to deal with this concern, *The Life and Letters of St. Paul*, written by the Reverend Dr. David Smith, was used to provide background and a source for non-canonical information. After a stellar record as a theological student, service as an active church pastor,

---

[1] The *Revised Standard Version* of the bible is used.

appointment as Professor of Theology at two universities, and lecturer at six others, Dr. Smith authored sixteen formidable books on Christianity. His *Life and Letters* is very helpful in any study of Paul's adventurous life.

Much is also owed to Professor William Barclay because of his wonderful series on each one of the Gospels and *The Acts of the Apostles*. To have *Acts* provided in "snack" segments immediately followed by his commentary is a boon to all students of the New Testament.

And last but not least, David Pawson, master of the spoken word, has provided Christians with a remarkable treasure in his masterpiece, *Unlocking The Bible*. He has left behind a complete set of keys for each book of the Old and the New Testaments. He has made reading them an adventure for the mind and spirit.

Speaking for the Defense: 1,970 years ago

The Apostle Paul was the Greatest Roman. He wrote 14 of the 27 books of the New Testament and led three lengthy missionary journeys throughout the areas now known as Greece and Turkey. This was done when Christianity was considered a new and revolutionary theology, strongly opposed by conservative leaders of his own culture and his own Jewish religion. He did all this to advise and instruct the new and struggling Christian churches of the first century. He suffered rejection, beatings, imprisonment, and stoning; all this in order to provide guidance to those early churches through the turbulent first years of their existence. His story is exciting, filled with danger, hope, disappointment, sadness, and then great joy. It is about real people, saints and sinners, heroes and pretenders; just like us. Yet all made in God's image, intended for His purposes.

As a young man, Paul was an extremely well educated leader of Judaism who despised the name of Jesus. As a mature man, he was a victorious teacher and champion of that same Jesus.

His writings reveal much of his ideas and his teachings, but little of his actions. To understand what he actually did, the best source is the Apostle Luke, his friend, physician, and author of *The Acts of the Apostles*. It would be well then, to examine the qualifications and motives of this man, Luke.

A Gentile Physician:

Luke was the only writer of the New Testament who was not a Jew; what the Jews called a Gentile. He was a Greek physician by training and profession, and a sometimes companion of Paul on his missionary journeys. He was far better educated than most of the other writers of the *New Testament*, and is one of the most precise and accurate of them in his testimonies. For example, of the six miracles of Jesus on which Luke comments, five of them dealt with healings, often including medical precision in his observations.

Like most other New Testament writers, Luke refrained from identifying his own role in his narrative, but his presence is frequently revealed when he changes appropriate pronouns from "he" to "we", and "them" to "us". These changes are subtle, but revealing of his presence.

A Paralegal Companion:

Luke spent four years of his life with Paul under difficult circumstances; two years with him awaiting trial in a Roman court in Caesarea, and two years in Rome where Paul was under house arrest, accused of the same crime with which Jesus was charged; the charge of treason against the Roman Empire.

Luke was an old man when he wrote about the adventures he shared with Paul. The story actually takes place when they were both young and engaged in taking on the world for a truly noble cause; the reconciliation between God and His creation. He tells it as if to defend Paul before an unbiased jury; as if it is a legal brief to describe what happened, when it happened, and why it happened. This brief is addressed to "Theophilus", a name which translates as "Friend of God". This could have been a defense lawyer in Rome, a particular judge, or merely a pseudonym for the court itself. That legal brief is known as *The Acts of the Apostles*.

The first five chapters are an introduction to Christianity, since this is very important to the defense.

The remaining twenty-three chapters describe much of Paul's life history, starting with his role as a persecutor of Christianity during its very beginning. This is to convince Theophilus of Paul's bona-fides as one who is fully aware of all the bad things claimed against Christianity.

It then describes Paul's own conversion to this new faith and the selfless dangers and risks he incurred as he sought to introduce this new theology to his Jewish brethren. Luke also takes care to honor Roman Justice as being fair in its administration, as demonstrated in Paul's early trials in Caesarea. It only makes sense that a good paralegal would not needlessly offend a Roman judge. Therefore, I think Luke can be seen as a precise and accurate historian as to the facts of Paul's life.

Some believe that Paul was acquitted on the charge of treason, and later arrested and spitefully murdered. However, the facts in Luke's legal brief are consistent with an acquittal by God's friend, Theophilus. However, there is no actual record as to the result of Paul's trial in Rome. It may have been one of the files that Diocletian burned.

PART II - SAUL

A Beginning: 1 AD

Our story begins with the birth of a son to a well educated and prosperous Jewish couple in Tarsus, an important city at the southeastern corner of present day Turkey. It was a significant city, already 4,000 years old when Pompey made it a part of the Roman Empire, just sixty-eight years before this story begins.

But the conquest of Cilicia, the region around Tarsus, had not changed the basic culture of the city. Even though it was famous as the meeting place of the Egyptian beauty Cleopatra and the heroic Roman, Mark Anthony, its culture was still Greek. That had been shaped centuries before by Alexander the Great when he spread Hellenistic culture as far as India.

The father of the boy born in Tarsus was a Roman citizen, which was very helpful to a Jewish family living under Roman law. Jerusalem was five hundred miles away and travel to its holy Temple required a long journey through other Roman Provinces. The father's plan was for his son to become a rabbi. He even hoped that his child might become a leader in the theocracy which Rome permitted to exist in Israel. Its capital was Jerusalem, and that's where his son's education would be completed.

The boy was given two names, one Jewish and one Gentile, meaning non-Jewish. His Jewish name was Saul and his Gentile, or Greek, name was Paul. This was common practice because the people of Israel lived two lives; one Jewish and one as a subject of Rome. While Aramaic was spoken in the home, Greek was the common language and the culture throughout the Roman Empire. This was one of the great benefits that came from Alexander's conquests.

The child's mother may have died shortly after he was born but apparently never shared in his achievements as he grew into his maturity as a member of the Sanhedrin, the highest court and governing body in Jerusalem. That success resulted from his father's plan to provide the best education for him, and this eventually led to his recognition as a Pharisee, one of the highest honors among all rabbis in Israel.

The educational system for this young Jewish boy is quite interesting. It began at age seven when he was sent to the local synagogue in Tarsus. There, he studied not only the scriptures but also the Hebrew language in order to read the Tanakh, the original books of the Bible which were written in Hebrew. This was not too difficult for him since Hebrew was quite similar to Aramaic.

While he spoke vernacular Greek in the streets, and was taught classical Greek in school, he was chastised if he read any secular form of Greek literature. However, despite that restriction during his boyhood, as a grown man he was found to be quite knowledgeable regarding Greek philosophy and rhetoric.

At age ten, his education began to focus on the law, both Biblical and Roman. This meant not only continuing to study at the synagogue, but probably attending the Academy of Tarsus. Understanding Roman law was particularly important for him because he had inherited Roman citizenship from his father.

At age thirteen, there was another significant step in his education. This had to do with his father's plan for him to become a rabbi. A rabbi was to be more than just a teacher of Israel; he was to be a blessing to the people. This meant that he would never charge a fee or accept gifts in compensation for his services as a rabbi. This meant that a rabbi had to earn his living in some other way. It was even said that "A father who fails to teach his son a craft, teaches robbery!"

In consequence, Saul spent the next two years as an apprentice learning a craft of his own choice, subject of course to the approval of his father. It might be a shoemaker, tailor, baker, carpenter, or mason. It could be any respectable line of work which would allow him to pay his own way. Saul's choice of a craft was directly affected by the geography in which he lived.

The region around Tarsus was the home of large herds of goats. As a result, Tarsus had become well known for the production of a strong fabric made from goat hair, which was especially suited for making tents. This tent fabric was exported and used throughout the Mediterranean for this purpose. Therefore, Saul and his father chose the craft of the tentmaker since it would be useful wherever he might travel. Tents were always in need of minor repairs, wherever one might be. Besides, tent making would not require heavy tools to carry with him, as would carpentry or masonry.

This idea, that a well-educated man should have a craft that could provide a livelihood, was a significantly different view toward manual labor than held by the Romans. Romans saw such crafts as beneath them, relegated to slaves who were trained to such purposes as their owner might require. These opposing views on manual labor are not archaic. Looking back a mere two hundred years reveals exactly the same distinctions in the United States.

By the time he was fifteen years old, Saul was ready to advance to the final stage of his formal education. This meant traveling five hundred miles to attend the Rabbinical College in Jerusalem. Fifteen may seem young for such profound philosophical studies, but it was quite appropriate in 16 AD. Two factors help to explain this; first, a lifetime was shorter back then, and a vocation needed to be started early. Second, education simply involved fewer topics to be studied.

This paradigm of advanced learning for young minds is also seen in the sixteenth century. In the early

1520s, John Calvin entered the University of Paris at sixteen. And even in the eighteenth century, our own George Washington was licensed as a surveyor by the College of William and Mary when he was only seventeen.

A Young Boy in Jerusalem: 16 AD

As a boy in Jerusalem on his own for the first time, Saul probably felt quite proud to roam through the busy streets and see the sites at his own time and discretion. On previous visits, sometimes lasting several days during the festivals, he was always in the company of his father and often with other travel companions. Those visits always left him a little disappointed, because he could not make his own choices of where to go and what to see.

Now he was older, and as he moved among the people, they seemed to sense that he was a new arrival at the college and they gave him a modicum of respect; something he had never known before. When he began his studies, he realized this bit of respect was warranted. His studies soon took up so much time that his sightseeing became a rare treat, and the people seemed aware of this and gave him even more respect.

His primary study was the Law, the Book of Precepts that formed the basis for Jewish customs and lifestyle. Next, he studied the words and biographies of the prophets and the early rabbis. He thrived on all of this, but it took a while to transition from his school in

Tarsus to the methods used here in the capital city. In Tarsus, the scarcity of written texts required that learning was done by rote; memorization as his teacher read a text. This left little time for discussion, whereas in Jerusalem, students were expected to think and to discuss a text intelligently!

Rather than merely listening to the Rabbi's words and then repeating them, he was now asked to explain the meaning of those texts which had already been lodged deep within his mind by rote. This sort of thinking was a new and wonderful experience for him, and he liked it. He began to understand why the people respected him.

His new teachers, the learned rabbis, divided thinking into two types; the Halachah and the Haggadah. The Halachah was a systematic definition and application of Jewish law, and then the reconciliation of inherent conflicts within it. This was no simple task, because of the hundreds of commandments, most of which were preceded by either "thou shall" or "thou shall not".

The second type of thinking, the Haggadah, served not only to tell the history of the Jews but also to explain it through midrash; using parables and allegory to clarify a text. One of his favorite teachers of midrash was Rabbi Gamaliel.[2] Years later, Saul would honor his teacher and his education, saying -

---

[2] Rabban Gamaliel, a leading authority in the Sanhedrin in the early first century AD.

"I am verily a man which am a Jew, born in Tarsus, a city in Cilicia, yet brought up in this city at the feet of Gamaliel, and taught according to the perfect manner of the law of the fathers, and was zealous toward God, as ye all are this day."[3]

"At the feet" was an appropriate description of his classes, since Gamaliel would sit upon a small raised platform while Saul and the other students sat on the floor around the great man. Gamaliel's grandfather had been the famous Hillel the Elder, who was also a teacher; the one who authored what is now called the Golden Rule.

Hillel worded this basic rule a little differently, but with the same message;

> "What is hateful to you, do not do to your fellow: this is the whole Torah; the rest is the explanation; go and learn."

Hillel's version had a tag-line, because he had challenged his students to explain the entire Torah, the first five books of scripture, to a man who would listen only as long as he could stand on one leg.

Thus Saul learned, and as he did, his respect for the law and all the commandments grew just as he did himself; strong and unshakable. When his training had

---

[3] Acts 22: 3

been completed, he very likely returned home to Tarsus as a rabbi; to serve his people, work at his craft, and continue to learn from the school of life.

A Young Rabbi in Tarsus: 20 AD

Saul's return to Tarsus meant the fulfillment not only of his own dreams but those of his father as well. Because of his father's wealth, he did not need to depend on tent-making. This allowed him to concentrate almost entirely on his role as a learned rabbi.

He kept up the appearance of a craftsman by maintaining a workspace on his father's property and buying enough of the heavy goat-hair canvas to establish it as a workplace. He had a shop, the tools, and the ability to mend tents. The only thing he lacked was customers.

The people knew he didn't need the work, and they were a little timid about placing a burden upon such a learned man; the brightest rabbi to graduate from the esteemed college in Jerusalem; a son of Tarsus, one with whom they had played as children, and the son of a man who could retaliate if they dared to complain about Saul's workmanship, or his prices. And who should be denied the right to complain?

Saul came to understand the reason for his lack of work. He didn't need the business, but he did need the self respect it would bring. So he moved his shop to a place closer to the synagogue, made an awning for it to demonstrate his craftsmanship, and acted cool but not disrespectful to his father while in the marketplace. His dad understood all this and took even greater pride in his son, not only as a rabbi, but as a man of business.

The business flourished. Saul soon had a reputation for good work at a fair price, and completed on time. He found that this also helped with the students in his classes on Torah and the sacred writings of the ancient rabbis. Students seemed to have added respect for him as a man of the world rather than merely a man of the book. In later years, this distinction would not be needed, but as a freshly minted rabbi, he had completed his first lesson in the school of life.

The World beyond Tarsus: 30 AD

Ten years had passed, and they had been good years; happy in the life he had chosen. He was serving both God and man as rabbi and craftsman. But he had recently begun to think that his passion for God and service to man were meant for a broader arena than the streets of Tarsus.

His success in Tarsus, and his interest in greater responsibility, was also becoming known to the Temple elders in Jerusalem. The passing years had brought a consistent flow of good reports; reports which added to the favorable opinions gained when Saul came to Jerusalem to observe the days of festivals. There had even been several occasions when he had been consulted on small matters of Temple policy. His fervor for the law was apparently unbounded, and his ability to defend it with logic and clarity was remarkable. He was now recognized in both Tarsus and Jerusalem as a rabbi of repute.

His time became equally divided between his home in Tarsus and his service in Jerusalem as a consultant to the Sanhedrin, the highest court of law and the legislature for all of Israel. This made him keenly aware of the greater world around him. For example, Rome was not ruled as a theocracy, like Israel. It was an empire ruled by a Caesar; Tiberius Caesar, who came to power two years before Saul had arrived in Jerusalem.

The first Caesar, Julius, had been the one who established this empire. What had long been a Republic, made up of city states in the Greek fashion, had become the stepping stone to greater personal power for an ambitious general. The Republic had lasted well over four hundred years; since the year 709 in the Roman calendar, or 4269 in the Jewish calendar. This new innovation in government, the Roman Empire, was only 75 years old and only on its third emperor; Tiberius.

The second Caesar, after Julius who had lasted for only a year, had been Caesar Augustus. He was the one who had begun the practice of using Julius' family name to identify as being the ruler. Augustus had done better, lasting 41 years, and he had instituted the Pax Romana, or Roman Peace, which lasted for the next 250 years. He was followed by Caesar Tiberius, who currently ruled in Rome, while allowing an Imperial Procurator to rule the entire Province of Judaea from Caesarea on the coast, and a Provincial Governor, Pontius Pilate, to administer military control from Jerusalem.

Pilate had held this office for just the last four years and was having trouble in balancing the need to maintain the military authority of Rome against the desire to keep good diplomatic relations with Caiaphas, the Jewish High Priest and leader of the Sanhedrin. This balance between military power and civil diplomacy was a political matter, and that's what Pontius Pilate really was; a politician.

He knew that the emperors in Rome kept a keen eye on all of their military governors throughout the empire, because peace was less expensive than war. But to men like Pilate, the cost of peace could demand payment in terms of their conscience, integrity, and place in history. Pilate knew all this, and accepted it with the politician's credo that it is better that the weak should suffer unfairly than the powerful be inconvenienced or even offended.

Subordinate to all of these Romans was a Jew, King Herod Agrippa II, who administered only a small part of the province. His role was not as a real 'King' but as an indigenous politician whose primary responsibility was to maintain the peace, the Pax Romana, among the Jewish people.

Saul gradually became aware of these relationships and motives. They become clearer to him and touched him more personally as his responsibilities moved from Tarsus to Jerusalem. He was now a member of the Sanhedrin, and was becoming aware of the intellectual compromises made all along the ladder of power that ran from Caiaphas to Herod, to Pilate, to Tiberius.

There was a clear example of this with a young preacher named John, who had lived a life of poverty and isolation in the desert wilderness. But then he started preaching in the streets and along the river Jordan, where he would baptize people who repented of their sinful ways. John had no power, and yet he rightly condemned Herod the Tetrarch for his incestuous marriage.

Saul saw this as foolish behavior on both sides; Herod because of his disregard for the laws of marriage, and John for his naivety. John had made his accusation against Herod loudly and in public. This made it a matter for the Sanhedrin. Therefore it had been up to the High Priest Caiaphas to step forward and take control of the matter. But he didn't, and John paid the price with his life.

It had not been up to Saul to get involved. He was still just a newcomer in Jerusalem and in no position to interfere. His only responsibility was simply to support and assist the High Priest in whatever was decided.

A New Calendar: 33 AD

While Saul had chosen not to interfere in the case of John the Baptist, he was definitely unhappy with the way it was handled. Setting aside the fact that the man was summarily executed under the order of Herod; even more importantly, it was a glaring act of defiance of Roman law, since Herod was simply not allowed to carry out a death penalty.

Saul was certainly not pro-Roman, but such defiance of Roman law was dangerous and could have brought repercussions against the authority still retained by the Sanhedrin. Caiaphas must have known this, so Saul simply ignored the matter and decided not to make an issue of Herod's behavior. Besides, John had certainly been a rabble rouser, and the Romans were probably just glad to see the last of him.

However, there was another case in which he did take an interest. There had been another preacher, a wandering pseudo rabbi called Jesus, who came from Nazareth and had no formal rabbinical training at all. There even may have been a connection with the dead baptizer, since John had claimed that his own mission had been to prepare the way for this new one. This apparent alliance would be unusual since most street preachers worked alone; intent only in fleecing the public in order to make a living with words rather than sweat-of-the-brow.

There was something else that was different. This Jesus had been circulating about Judaea, and even troublesome Samaria, for about three years. Saul was actually surprised that he himself had never seen this imposter during the holy days in Jerusalem. There must have been several times when they were both in the city, but Saul had never laid eyes on him. "No great loss," he thought, "happily we traveled in different circles!"

But this Jesus had become a more known quantity. He had attracted large crowds, and had entertained gullible people with acts such as curing hypochondriacs, and providing secreted food and drink to his audience as if by magic. Far worse, he then challenged the Pharisees in the Temple itself; claiming all sorts of things, such as the authority to forgive sin, and in one instance at a synagogue in Caesarea, he even claimed to be the foretold Messiah.

Such things were not new, of course. There had other fakers through the years, but the people had soon seen through the trickery and just stopped feeding the imposters and they just faded away. The Sanhedrin and the Romans merely bided their time, and conducted perfunctory investigations if deemed necessary. This frightened off most of the obstinate fakers, but this one was different. He persisted until the High Priest decided that something more was needed.

As a result, a bargain was made with a follower of Jesus, one Judas Iscariot, to divulge a place where the man could be found at night and whisked before an abbreviated meeting of the Sanhedrin. This should have frightened him into fleeing Jerusalem to save himself.

Saul was rather disappointed at the details concerning the treatment of Jesus during this process. Caiaphas knew, or more likely had known as a young rabbi, that there were laws which prohibited any arrest at night unless the crime specifically involved violence or thievery committed during the night.

There was also the matter of witnesses. A lawful conviction would require at least two male witnesses to the crime, and Saul later learned that this rule had not been satisfied. But these details became moot when the trial had gotten out of hand. Jesus had openly claimed to be the Son of God, the Messiah; directly in front of the High Priest himself and several members of the Sanhedrin.

Caiaphas had torn his garments, the clear recognition of having witnessed blasphemy. This sealed the matter. What had been intended merely to frighten the poor demented man had instead turned into something that was beyond the pale. Caiaphas had so intimidated the man that he had truly blasphemed within the highest court of Israel. This was something that required a sentence of death as a blasphemer.

This was serious, and Caiaphas knew he must deal with it. Furthermore, he knew that, because Herod had mishandled the baptizer affair, he had better pay attention to Roman law lest Pilate further restrict Jewish autonomy. He therefore had Jesus immediately taken from the Sanhedrin to Pilate for permission to have the sentence executed. This was required because while the Sanhedrin could pass judgment, it could not order temple guards to execute the man. Only the Romans could do that, and they did it cruelly and expertly.

Pilate, awakened from his sleep, had examined the prisoner, and decided that no Roman law had been broken. This, despite the Jewish claim that Jesus was a revolutionary who planned to establish his own kingdom. However, Roman politics then entered the picture.

Pilate saw the Jewish charge about a new kingdom as an impossible subterfuge, used only to provide cover for their narrow-minded religious motives. So Pilate, upon finding that Jesus was from a town in Galilee, played the obvious political card. He had Jesus taken to Herod Agrippa the Tetrarch of Galilee as the appropriate ruler to judge a Galilean. Pilate had no intention to help Caiaphas solve a dispute among the Jews.

It was well past midnight when Jesus was brought before Herod, who was in the midst of a night of revelry. It was, after all, a time of festivities to enjoy the holy days. Not having the wit to deal with a political contest between Caiaphas and Pilate, this son of Herod the Great obfuscated. He merely challenged Jesus to entertain his guests with a miracle, and failing in this, he returned the prisoner to Pilate.[4]

By this time, dawn had broken, and a raucous crowd had gathered outside of Pilate's palace. Pilate was now boxed in. He would lose face if he gave in to the High Priest's demand, but the crowd had been aroused and a riot might ensue if he did not. So he tried to satisfy them with a compromise. He had Jesus scourged; a beating that could prove deadly. This would dispose of the problem without showing deference to Caiaphas.

However, Pilate's compromise didn't work. Jesus was horribly whipped, but he lived, and yet the crowd still cried for Jesus to be crucified. Pilate then offered a last-minute option to the frenzied crowd. Pilate was willing to free either a well-known murderer named Barabbas or Jesus; but not both. One must die. Without hesitation, the crowd, in unreasoned rage, shouted, "Crucify Jesus!"

On Thursday[5], April 2nd of 33 AD, Jesus was taken beyond the city gates to the place of execution and crucified on a Roman cross. Pilate had allowed it, and then literally washed his hands to show his contempt for his political rival, Caiaphas. Therefore, Caesar Tiberius was not disturbed by the report of a riot in Jerusalem;

---

[4] Luke 23:7-11
[5] David Pawson taught that a "Double Sabbath" explains the crucifixion on Thursday. See Wikipedia, "Crucifixion of Jesus"; Chronology.

because there was no riot. It had been avoided by his appointed military commander.

Saul's Mission: Late Spring, 33 AD

Caiaphas soon learned that the teachings of Jesus had taken root in the minds and hearts of far too many Jews to be ignored. Thankfully, and with Roman cooperation, the situation had been dealt with quickly. Jesus had been executed. Nevertheless, there were many in the city who persisted in claims that he had somehow survived the crucifixion, as if the Romans had failed in their role as executioners.

More significant to the High Priest was that in several synagogues, people continued to revere the parables taught by this Jesus. His followers, or disciples, intended to honor his memory by preaching about his teachings. Caiaphas could not understand this. The death of Jesus had been intended to serve as a warning to them that blasphemy would never be tolerated; even by well-intentioned but ignorant fishermen.

But Caiaphas learned, and was concerned, that a well- trained clerk named Mathew had become connected with the group. He was well educated and had worked for the Romans as a tax-collector, which made him detested by the Jews. Yet he was now accepted by this Jesus sect. This raised a concern that the heresy may have infected even the more sophisticated people of the city.

Saul knew that Caiaphas and several others in the Sanhedrin were worried about this, and saw it as an opportunity to establish himself as a pro-active Pharisee; not the type who said little and did even less. So he approached Caiaphas to ask if there were a service which he might provide to ease the burdens of the High Priest.

"I appreciate your offer; very much, Saul. As a young man among your elders, you may see my duties as varied and quite time-consuming. But I assure you that I am quite able to perform these duties. Indeed, they do include more than you might imagine, and the complexity would make you cross-eyed!"

This old man is not about to be eased out of his position. Not quite yet, you ambitious young scoundrel.

"Saul, I know you to be very bright and passionate in the law, and your home is in - - Tarsus? I believe that is the place? I hear such good reports of your work there. Now then, do you have some special talent which may be of service to me?"

The old man leaned forward as he said this, as if to help a child form the words needed to express his needs.

Saul sensed that he may have stubbed his toe in stepping so far forward. But his plan was a bold one; to take this conflict directly into the synagogues, and if need be into the streets where the poor and downtrodden were attracted by anything that was new and might allow the possibility of change.

"No, nothing that one might consider 'special'. But I have studied under Gamaliel, and I have an inclination toward rhetoric which could be useful to identify heresy where the ignorant see only free bread and wine."

"Yes, such a talent is always useful in a young rabbi. I myself studied under Gamaliel's grandfather you know; Hillel the Elder."

Saul nodded respectfully, but was surprised to find that even a High Priest could feel the need to impress a simple rabbi from a distant city. Then he smiled inwardly, realizing that Caiaphas was obviously intimidated by his difficulties with this new sect.

So Saul made his point. "Possibly I could go out among the people and restore them to sanity through the use of logical debate? We both know the power of debate when used by one proficient in the law."

Caiaphas did not respond immediately. He did what he often did when confronted with an idea which was very good, but not his own. He raised his chin, paused as if in deep thought, then answered almost dismissively.

"Yes; an excellent thought. I'm sure that if you spent some time out in the streets, you might achieve more than we who must serve at the Holy of Holies. Yes, Saul! Go to the streets and I do hope you can claim victories among these Nazarenes."

The High Priest clearly meant this as the end of the interview. Saul bowed and left respectfully, but not deterred by Caiaphas' attempt to belittle his offer of help. He had achieved what he really wanted; relief from Temple responsibilities. This would allow him the time and authority to lock horns with those who traded in heresy.

Saul Begins His Campaign: Early Summer, 33 AD

Among those synagogues where the heretical views were discussed, there were two distinct types; some attended by people of the Jewish race, and others in which the congregation was rather Hellenistic; heavily influenced by Greek culture. There had even been a time, prior to the Romans, when the office of High Priest itself had been held by a Hellenist as a matter of heritage.

All of these synagogues used the Septuagint, or Greek translation, of the scriptures. This was a translation from the Hebrew language and had been done almost three hundred years ago. The purpose had been to facilitate the growth of Judaism throughout the great empire that had already been established by Alexander the Great.

These particular synagogues, those now suspected of heresy, were showing an increased interest in works of charity. This was apparently based upon the parables of Jesus. Moreover, they soon began referring to themselves as Nazarenes since Jesus came from that town.

The Nazarenes did not see this as a denial of their Judaism but only as an expression of their support of the new teachings which were a fulfillment of the Jewish Bible. In particular, Jesus had performed a miraculous feeding of multitudes when no food seemed to be available.

In imitation of this, they undertook charitable programs to provide help to the neediest of all; the widows and orphans of their community. But it soon became apparent that this program required at least the rudiments of organization. This could have been expected, considering that two heritages were involved. Disputes occurred between Jews and Hellenists as to the fairness in the distribution of food.

This led to the creation of a board of Deacons, seven men selected not only for their administrative talent, but for their spiritual gifts as well. Among these was a man called Stephen. He was a kind and a gentle man, and yet he had a reputation for persuasive speaking. This became apparent in various synagogues where he spoke in witness to the teachings of Jesus. This, of course, made him a target for Saul's mission to stamp out what he viewed as heresy.

Persuasive or not, Stephen should have been no match for Saul. Saul had been trained in the law by the best minds in Jerusalem, whereas Stephen had no training in debate and spoke only from what he had learned about Jesus and from his own experience within the Nazarene community. Of the several congregations to whom he spoke, the one best attended was in the southeastern part of the city, located across the Valley of the Kidron from the Mount of Olives; the closest synagogue to the Garden where Jesus had prayed.

Therefore, Saul chose this as the place where he would begin his campaign. His plan was to undermine the movement by challenging the heresy with logical debate rather than violence, as used by Caiaphas. The High Priest had seriously misjudged their enemies, and he had foolishly aroused the sympathy of the poor and humble who had lost their leader. Saul would defeat them with gentle logic. And an opportunity to do this came one evening when Stephen was to discuss what he had learned from Matthew, the ex tax-collector.

"Yes," Stephen said, "Mathew inspired me! He said we Hellenist Jews are just the beginning. He recalled Jesus' words, saying that the good news of his kingdom will be preached throughout the entre world! [6] And we should not fear to say this, even here in Jerusalem."

---

[6] Matthew 24: 13

Saul sat at the rear of the gathering to establish his separation from Stephen. Also, he needed room to stand and be seen when he spoke, so that people could see his face. He would be easily recognized as the well known Pharisee; unlike Stephen, who was known only among these adherents to a new sect. Now Saul seized upon Stephen's obvious call for insurrection.

"Wait, Stephen! Do you say we should not fear to propose a new kingdom right here in Jerusalem? You know this Jesus was executed for announcing such a plan for a new kingdom that would replace the rule of Herod. That would challenge even the Romans! He speaks of 'his kingdom'; indeed! Does he expect this group of farmers and shepherds to subdue a garrison of the Tenth Legion?"

He had captured the attention of Stephen's listeners and they turned to see who had spoken. He noticed their raised eyebrows, showing a return to rationality.

He continued, "Recall the words of Moses when he said 'For you are a people holy to the LORD your God, and the LORD has **chosen** you to be a people for his own possession, out of all the peoples that are on the face of the earth.'[7] You see my friends, we are a **chosen** people. For a thousand years, we have remained a chosen nation, like no other. And clearly we should remain so."

---

[7] Deuteronomy 14: 2

The audience, now enlightened by this learned rabbi, turned to Stephen for a response. Stephen sensed that his answer must not refute, but build upon Saul's argument. He spoke while seated, according the custom.

"Yes Rabboni, you have spoken correctly. But that scripture also says, 'And if you obey the voice of the LORD your God, being careful to do all his commandments which I command you this day, the LORD your God will set you high above all the nations of the earth.' [8]

"And now my fellow Nazarenes, knowing we have failed to obey, now we have the words of Jesus who told John, 'A new commandment I give to you, that you love one another; even as I have loved you.' " [9]

"Blasphemy! Who is this man who takes on the role of God? Who can create a 'new commandment' but God alone?" Saul stood with his arms spread in the style of the Greeks, realizing that Stephen was craftier than he had expected. Now, he was convinced in the rightness of his cause. This heresy must be stopped at any cost!

But Stephen went on, "Jesus is our Nazarene! He does not deny the law of the Torah, but is one who says like Hillel the Elder, 'That which is hateful to you, do not do to your fellow. That is the whole Torah.' Jesus has lived a life that speaks the Words of Hillel! He would

---

[8] Deuteronomy 28: 1
[9] John 13: 34

share the whole of the Torah, the Commandments, our God, and our love for one another with everyone. Don't you see that, Saul?"

At this point, the crowd was embroiled in controversy. It was useless for either Stephen or Saul to continue, so Saul left before any violence might befall him, being the stranger in the meeting. He was shocked at the ease with which his words from scripture had been turned against him. This danger might demand greater attention than he had thought.

Greater Attention from Saul:

Saul had been taken by surprise. He had never experienced defeat and embarrassment such as happened with Stephen. His previous experience in debate had been with other rabbis or teachers who had been friendly to his views, and to him. Stephen was not. And how had this untrained amateur theologian acquired such skill? He had spoken as one possessed. As if a foreign spirit had shaped his thoughts. As if being the children of Abraham were as nothing at all; as if their history and inheritance should be simply passed out to the uncircumcised world.

Two days later, Stephen was scheduled to speak at another synagogue and the public expected Saul to appear also, to reclaim his dignity as a Pharisee. But this time Saul would be ready for him. This time he would buttress his position with the authority of the High Priest of Israel and with the wisdom of his own teacher Gamaliel, who had been taught by the renowned Hillel.

The meeting began with prayer, led by an older rabbi who carefully said nothing that might be misunderstood as an endorsement for either side in the controversy; a dispute which hung like a dark cloud over the entire room.

Then a young man rose to make introductions, almost apologetically, in the hope that a peaceful discussion could be enjoyed by all. Then unexpectedly, Saul found himself being introduced as the first speaker so that he could present the view of someone in authority who questioned the teachings which had so excited these Nazarenes.

Surprised as he was, Saul gladly saw this as his opportunity to assume the role of the wiser, more educated leader. He therefore spoke slowly, almost condescendingly to the group, thanking them for this opportunity to represent the opinions of the Temple leaders.

"High Priest Caiaphas, as his father before him, has always sought to fulfill the great responsibility of preserving the well being and the faith of all our people."

He then continued, to point out several well-known instances to show the wisdom of Caiaphas. The final example was a direct quotation of Caiaphas that had been spoken to the Sanhedrin about Jesus. "You do not understand that it is expedient for you that one man should die for the people, and that the whole nation should not perish." [10]

This caused a wave of concern among the audience, and Saul noticed Stephen's face go pale for a moment. But then he went on with what he considered his final argument.

"I shall conclude my remarks simply with an apology to the great Hillel, who was quoted unjustly at a recent meeting attended by some of you. Hillel lived and taught long before my time, but a student of that great man was my own teacher. And despite the cleverness of this man Stephen, here present, I think I am in a position to represent the view of Gamaliel, my own teacher in the Torah. And I am certain that if Gamaliel were here, he would never condone such heresy as I have heard from Stephen and others of his faction."

The room was stunned into silence; Stephen did not rise until Saul had seated himself, smiling with the confidence of a shepherd who had brought his sheep through a dangerous storm. Then Stephen, who remained seated, spoke humbly; almost regretfully.

"Rabbi Saul; good friends and followers. I have not heard this saying of Caiaphas about the death of Jesus. And it may be that the High Priest meant his words

---

[10] John 11: 49 - 51

differently than I understand them tonight. But I do believe that indeed, Jesus did die for all the Sanhedrin; for our whole nation, and indeed for the sins of the world.[11] It is something which only God could do for us."

Now there came a murmur of agreement from the audience. Stephen paused to allow his words to reach their full impact.

"And apparently, Saul, you have not heard the latest words of your teacher, Rabbi Gamaliel. He spoke this very afternoon, when Peter and some other men had been brought before the Sanhedrin to be warned and threatened by the High Priest Caiaphas."

Stephen then told Saul, and everyone, what Gamaliel had said to the Sanhedrin that very day.

"But a Pharisee in the council named Gamaliel, a teacher of the law, held in honor by all the people, stood up and ordered the men to be put outside for a while. And he said to them, 'Men of Israel, take care what you do with these men.' [12]

"Your teacher Gamaliel then recounted past times when men were needlessly killed and others scattered to no account. Then he concluded, 'So in the present case I tell you, keep away from these men and let them alone; for if this plan or this undertaking is of men, it will

---
[11] John 11: 51 - 52
[12] Acts 5: 35

fail; but if it is of God, you will not be able to overthrow them. You might even be found opposing God!' "[13]

And here Stephen ended the meeting, looking with sympathy upon Saul as the people rushed forward to thank him for his refutation of Saul's attack upon their newfound faith. But Saul was furious in his mind.

Saul's Fury Unleashed: 33 to 36 AD

Stephen's victory in debate was recognized by Caiaphas as merely a setback, but it was deeply resented by Saul. The High Priest was above the fray, and felt no personal defeat. His inclination was to move forward by using the same tactic he had used against Jesus. The new threat, this upstart Stephen, would be watched and brought to trial on whatever charge seemed most winnable.

Saul, however, was not as wise in politics as was Caiaphas. Saul was still young enough to think that his success as a rabbi depended entirely upon his ability as a prosecutor of Mosaic Law; and he had failed. Now, he hated Stephen on a personal level. The debates with Stephen had been based upon the laws of Moses. But now, Stephen had become Saul's personal enemy.

Caiaphas, tempered by his years of experience, was quite willing to allow Saul the task of cleansing Israel. Thus, Saul's penchant for activity and meticulous

---
[13] Acts 5: 38-39

attention to detail came to the fore. He soon perfected the finding and punishment of Nazarenes, without regard to sex, age, or the need for compassion.

Inevitably, this resulted in the coarseness of women and children being caught up in a first century pogrom. The most that can be said for Saul is that he at least felt a sense of embarrassment. Dragging a mother from her home and putting her on trial because she had persisted in ignoring warnings was clearly a hateful act. So he refrained from executing his policies in person, but his policies continued. They lasted far beyond the time he had thought would be needed to conclude his project of persecution.

The Entrapment of Stephen:

Four long years had passed, and still the persecution went on. And yet, Stephen had prospered in his role as a witness for Jesus. He had been elected to a committee of seven, called Deacons, who administered the charitable affairs of the Nazarenes.

Then there came a day that was inevitable. From the very beginning, Stephen had been too significant a person to be attacked physically. Any violence done to him would have merely aroused sympathy for him and his cause. The years of determined harassment upon his congregation had not been enough to stop him. It was time for direct action against Stephen the man.

Saul's agents had been ordered to attend services at what had become known as the synagogue of Cilicia, attended by Hellenistic Jews, mainly from Ephesus and Tarsus. Saul had selected this place to be watched, thinking that his own connection with Tarsus might sway people to his side in the effort to take down Stephen. They took note of anything Stephen said that could result in formal charges against him.

When the collection of evidence convinced Saul that a case could be proven, he had Stephen arrested and brought before the Sanhedrin for trial on two charges. Each charge amounted to heresy.

The first charge was that he disputed the Temple and the Holy of Holies as being the dwelling place of God. Second, he taught that the Law of Moses was not the only sure means to God's favor. There were ample witnesses available to prove these charges and High Priest Caiaphas demanded of Stephen, "Is this so?" [14]

Stephen had proudly smiled when the question had been put to him; proud because Jesus had faced the very same question. Then, when the Sanhedrin asked for a response to specific questions, his face shined as the face of an angel being asked to explain the history and beliefs of the Jewish people.

As to the charge that he disparaged the Temple, he pointed out that their history had begun with Father

---

[14] Acts 7: 1

Abraham, who had made the founding Covenant with God; making them His special people. And this had happened 2,000 years before the Temple was even built. No physical Temple had been needed to "house" God. And then, he reminded them all of God's words to Moses as he stood on Mount Sinai saying, "Take off the shoes from your feet, for the place where you are standing is holy ground." [15] And there was no Temple there!

Now the temper of the court became heated with anger, and Stephen feared that they might never allow him to speak in answer to the second charge; and he was correct in this fear. So he dealt with them even more directly, speaking from the prophets.

"Yet the Most High does not dwell in houses made with hands; as the prophet says, 'Heaven is my throne, and earth my footstool. What house will you build for me, says the Lord, or what is the place of my rest? Did not my hand make all these things?'

"You stiff-necked people, uncircumcised in heart and ears, you always resist the Holy Spirit. As your fathers did, so do you. Which of the prophets did not your fathers persecute? And they killed those who announced beforehand the coming of the Righteous One, whom you have now betrayed and murdered, you who received the law as delivered by angels and did not keep it." [16]

---

[15] Acts 7: 33, and Exodus 3:5
[16] Acts 7: 48-53

The Stoning of Stephen:

Stephen's indictment was not merely against the Sanhedrin that sat before him, but of all the previous Sons of Abraham who for centuries had condemned the prophets, like John, the one who made straight the way for the Son of God. Saul felt the sting of Stephen's words personally, since he had been foremost of those who persecuted the Nazarenes who announced Jesus.[17]

The eyes of his judges grew red with rage as he finished speaking and they rose up as one to shout their protests. Stephen knew what his words meant for himself. He merely raised his eyes like a man in the midst of a storm to better see the first rays of the sun.

His lips moved, but he made no protest against his attackers. They shouted curses and covered their ears as they descended upon him. He and all who seized him knew the penalty to be paid, but it could not be done there within the high chamber in which they met. Such things were done outside the gates of their sacred city.

So they dragged him, hardly visible among those who held fast on him lest their unresisting victim should rise up and defeat their purpose. When they reached the place where stoning had happened many times before, and an ample supply of rocks lay close at hand, they began the hideous ceremony of execution.

---

[17] Acts 26: 10

Saul was there amongst them, but while he had instigated the collection of evidence against Stephen, he still considered himself as a just man of the law. But the law required a trial and conviction, not a mob killing. He stopped to think, just short of reaching the stoning pit.

He believed in the evidence he had assembled, but he also believed that Stephen had been truthful in his indictment of his judges. As stone clenched fists were raised to kill Stephen, Saul raised his eyes to the light blue sky above and fleetingly pictured himself as a defender of the accused, and imagined himself gaining the poor man's acquittal.

But then he looked down and saw that robes had been left at his feet to avoid the chance of becoming stained with blood. Stephen was kneeling now, bent and submissive as to God. More stones descended, and he fell forward and his lips moved slowly as he fell asleep.

Saul's Uncertainty:

Saul was deeply shocked and permanently affected by the death of Stephen. Who would not be! The rain of stones, some too large to be held in one hand, required two hands to be raised and crashed down upon him!

Saul had seen dumb animals treated more kindly when sacrificed at the Temple. He was no stranger to the idea of purposely killing a living thing, but he recalled that even the lambs had fought back against their pain.

Stephen's acquiescence at the execution pit, and the expensive robes left at his feet, had raised an unfamiliar feeling within him. It was the sharp sting of doubt.

He had felt that sting before; but not very often. When he had first come to Jerusalem as a student, and had debated with the older students. And then again in discussions with his teachers. But as his knowledge of the law had deepened, he had become more sure-footed in debate. He had become secure in his knowledge of God, and doubt had become a thing of the past.

But when Stephen had defended himself before the Sanhedrin, he had spoken not as one whose knowledge of God came from debate, but from personal acquaintance. When Stephen spoke, he had spoken to the intellectual guardians for the teachings of Moses as if they were children who had gotten lost in a forest of stout trees; so covered with leaves that God's sun was blocked out.

But Saul's education had been in logic, not inspiration; reality, not delusion; discipline instead of understanding. Stephen had willingly declared his own death sentence when he spoke his blasphemy! And of course such madness must be stopped.

But the madness was becoming worse. Followers of "The Way", which is how they now referred to themselves[18], were spreading throughout the province; to

---

[18] Acts 13: 9

Cilicia in the north, and even to Egypt in the south. The harsher they were punished, the further they scattered, which meant that the heresy flowed even further.

It was useless to seek help from the Romans; they thought their emperor who sat in Rome was a God, and they maintained their "Roman Peace" by allowing ignorant provincials to worship whatever gods took their fancy. The Jews were the only people who knew and understood the great truth of a single, unique God. It was their responsibility therefore, and Saul's duty, to stamp out this other "Way".

The Way to Damascus:

Caiaphas was easily convinced that an envoy should be sent to distant cities to combat the problem. Antioch in Syria, a nesting place of Greek worldliness, was especially in need of correction. And since Saul had asked for this role, he was naturally the one to go there.

In planning his campaign, Saul chose Damascus to be his first stop on the way to Antioch. This meant forgoing the more comfortable coastal passage aboard a well founded vessel, but Damascus could not be ignored. It was a crossroads city where new ideas could be effectively spread; or stopped. Besides, by planning the expedition as a land voyage, it became a simple matter to expand it to include a visit to his family home in Tarsus.

Paul's father still lived there, and would be happy to see him. He also had a sister, but she now lived in Jerusalem with her son.[19] But it was his father whom he now longed to see; to thank him once again for his understanding during those early days when he had feigned coolness toward his father in the market place of Tarsus.

Saul's own marriage had been delayed beyond the usual time for Jewish men to remain single. The Jewish custom was for men to get married quite young, but the great Maimonides had created an "exception" for law students. However, after graduation, the pressure had resumed and Saul got married. This had allowed him to accept the great honor of admission to the Sanhedrin. The theory being that only married men should create and administer the laws, since love and marriage would bring greater maturity.

There is nothing recorded concerning his marriage, which indicates that it may have ended, whatever the reason, prior to or slightly after he began his role as persecutor of the Nazarenes. This may have resulted in an embitterment which led him to later advise those without a spouse to remain single, as he had done.[20]

In any case, a visit to his father would be a welcome bonus after his responsibilities in Damascus.

---

[19] Acts 23: 16; Years later, this sister's son, saved Paul's life during a plot to assassinate him. See page 105.
[20] I Cor. 7: 8

Saul Begins His Journey of a Lifetime:

This was a journey on official business, so Saul had no problem in assembling what was needed for a safe and comfortable trip. It meant four nights on the road, two of which would be in the homes of people Saul already knew, one night at an inn, and one at a hillside campsite east of the Sea of Galilee. This required a camel to carry the tenting and cooking equipment, while he and his secretary would ride horses, as would two Temple guards.

The road was a safe one, being well traveled between two important cities; it bustled with tradesmen and manufactured goods. The Temple guards were needed more to serve as swift messengers than as protectors. Nonetheless, it was wise to have two swords readily available, and then there was always the chance that a significant prisoner might require immediate transport back to Jerusalem.

Since the camel driver and his beast traveled more slowly than the horses, they had to leave earlier each morning to arrive at the day's destination well before the official party. This problem was somewhat eased because Saul would often suggest a spell of walking during the day since he was not accustomed to the saddle.

It was the third night on the road when they made camp high on a hill overlooking the Sea of Galilee, which lay ten miles to the west. It provided a lovely sight, with the setting sun finding a way through gray clouds to glimmer across the widest stretch of the huge lake.

It had been a long day. They had crossed the Jordan River about noon, and thus left the Sea of Galilee behind. From there they had followed the road that climbed up to their campsite. It was waiting for them, all prepared just off the roadway.

Saul was tired, so he ate little supper and wanted only peaceful rest. The road traffic had dwindled to a lonely shepherd bringing his few sheep back from the upland grass, and Saul's thoughts went back to his days as a young rabbi in Tarsus. Those were the peaceful days, and like that young shepherd, his life had centered upon caring for the needs of others, and he suddenly remembered how rewarding and joyful that life had been. Slowly, he became aware that his shoulders had relaxed and that the tiredness was flowing out of him.

"Sir? You asked me to prepare a list of names; the people to be searched for when we reach Damascus." His aide's voice pulled him back to his official duties. He was asked if this would be a good time to review the list.

"No." He looked again at the fading sunset and heard the distant voice of the shepherd scolding a stray lamb back to the flock.

"No. We still have one more night before Damascus. We can do it then. I know it must be done."

He paused and glanced at one of the tired soldiers, then added, "And of course I will do what must be done."

Saul Reaches Damascus:

The following day passed uneventfully, and they had reached the comfortable home of his good friend just twenty miles short of Damascus. They had talked late into the evening, explaining his mission and asking his friend's advice on how to proceed, since this would be his first visit to Damascus. His aide had produced the list of names and he was rather surprised that the list contained several prominent people who were known to his host.

At noon the next day, Damascus was in sight and Saul would soon be in the ancient city. He was refreshed by the comfort of his friend's home and the clear mountain air. He was ready for whatever might come.

He and his secretary now walked together as the Temple Guards, still in their saddles, slowly rode ahead. They had been late on getting started because of Saul's reluctance to leave the comfort of his friend's home, but this last day's travel was shorter than usual and they had already completed half of it.

"Your list will be a revelation to our friends in the city! You've done a fine job and it will make our stay a very successful one. And I'll see that you're well rewarded for helping me with what needs to be done."

An instant flash of light surround him as he spoke, and he found himself laying prone across the roadway, clearing the white road dust from his lips. He raised his head to hear a clear voice speaking to him.

"Saul, Saul, why do you persecute me?"

Stunned into submission, Saul raised his head to ask who was speaking.

"I am Jesus, whom you are persecuting; but rise and enter the city, and you will be told what you are to do." [21]

Those about him looked to find the one to whom Saul spoke, but there was no one within shouting distance. Saul struggled to get up, thinking he had been blinded by the sun. His secretary helped him, and the soldiers surrounded him with swords partly drawn. But there was no one to be seen. Saul wiped his eyes and realized that he still could not see clearly. But it didn't seem to matter to him. He felt a sense of contentment that made little sense. He acted as though he had somehow grown a new sense that replaced his ability to see.

Even as the voice had spoken the words "*I am*", something new had begun; as though just those two words had infused his body. It was the return of a peace which had left him on that frightful day when he had left

---

[21] Acts 9: 3-6

his home to become a student in Jerusalem. That was the day he felt he would never be with his father again.

Damascus was now a new beginning for him. He stretched out his hands for help, not knowing which way to go. The soldiers were confused; unsure what service they could provide, but his assistant clasped both of his arms and silently hoped the blindness might pass. But it did not, and Saul was guided with tentative steps toward the old city. Now, as he was led by the hand, Saul wondered, had the Messiah come and he had been just too blind to see it?

His thoughts whirled as he walked in darkness, but he was certain of one thing; he was no longer alone. He was closer to God than he had ever been, and thoughts of his father and his lost wife came easily, but now with the tears he had refused to shed lest they melt his vindictive heart. Now they flowed easily and filled his beard.

Medhat Basha:

Damascus is the oldest capital in the world. Its streets had been designed by a Greek architect[22] in the fifth century BC. He had used the grid system, with streets that were perfectly straight and perpendicular to one another. The most significant street ran from west to east and was known as Straight Street. Today, it is known by the name Medhat Basha.

---

[22] Hippodamus, 498 - 408 BC

When the party reached the outermost wall of the city, Saul asked to be taken to the home of a man called Judas, who lived on the street called Straight. The previous evening, this man had been recommended to Saul as one who might be helpful in his search for heretics. But now, Saul was in no condition to do this; physically or mentally. He was certain that God had now chosen him for some other purpose.

In another part of the city there lived a man named Ananias, who was a stranger to this Judas, but whose name was quite likely included among those on the list carried by Saul's secretary. This was because Ananias was a Jew and a follower of The Way. He lived in fear, as did many others because they were already aware of Saul's coming.

Now, an intricate and amazing sequence of events took place which precludes any human planning. The wondrous works of God are often accomplished in what appear to be mysterious ways; the better to make clear the presence of His hand.

The man named Ananias, who was a stranger to Judas in whose home Saul rested, experienced a vision in which God spoke to him saying; *"Ananias."*

Immediately knowing the source of this voice, Ananias answered as a true believer; "Here I am, Lord." With no idea what might be required of him, he was instantly willing to serve.

"Rise and go to the Street Called Straight, and inquire at the house of Judas for a man of Tarsus called Saul; for behold, he is praying, and he has seen a man named Ananias come in and lay his hands on him so that he may regain his sight." [23]

This confused poor Ananias, for he had heard things about this Judas of Damascus and was skeptical of him. But of Saul from Tarsus, there was no uncertainty. "Lord, I have heard from many about this man, how much evil he has done to thy saints at Jerusalem; and he has authority from the High Priests to bind all who call upon thy name." [24] Ananias was willing to serve God, but apparently he thought the Lord might not be fully aware. So God spoke again.

"Go, for he is a chosen instrument of mine to carry my name before the Gentiles and kings and the sons of Israel; for I will show him how much he must suffer for the sake of my name." [25]

Ananias needed no further encouragement, and he departed immediately to find the home of Judas. There, he faithfully followed the instructions which the Lord had provided concerning Saul.

He laid his hands upon Saul as if he were a member of The Way saying, "Brother Saul, the Lord

---

[23] Acts 9: 10 - 12
[24] Acts 9: 13 - 14
[25] Acts 9: 15 - 16

Jesus who appeared to you on the road by which you came, has sent me that you may regain your sight and be filled with the Holy Spirit." [26]

Saul was baffled by this stranger's knowledge of his experience on the road, and that he had come to lay loving hands upon him. But he accepted all this as a validation of God's will, and the blinding scales of hate and anger fell from his eyes completely. He had been blind but now could see, was baptized, took food and regained his strength.[27]

The Rejection of Saul in Damascus:

Saul's conversion was miraculous, but he was still Saul. He spoke in the synagogues of Damascus, proclaiming the miracle of his experience, but the Jews were more amazed by his story than convinced of its truth. His reputation as a persecutor was too well known to be ignored. The death of Stephen reminded them that their own lives could be forfeited by believing him. He was well known as a clever man with the use of words, but words not supported with evidence made a weak foundation for belief.

Some believed him, but there were others who were viciously suspicious, and they plotted against him. These others saw his "conversion" merely as a way to entrap them; to bind them, and take them to Jerusalem for

---

[26] Acts 9:17
[27] Acts 9: 18 - 19

trial and death. So the Jews of Damascus were of two minds and could not reconcile their differences.

The plotters decided they could not risk any more time debating the matter. Unwilling to trust him and full of revenge, they laid plans to kill him. But killing him inside the city could defeat any hope for acceptance for their sect, and they feared the charge of murder. So they planned to wait for his return to Jerusalem; to overtake him on the road and kill him there. Then his death could be blamed on thieves along the highway.

Knowing the city gates were now under constant watch by the plotters, Saul's supporters convinced him that he dare not risk a public departure from the city. He agreed that his story would never be accepted in Damascus, but hoped that he would be accepted back in Jerusalem. He therefore submitted to a plan of escape from the city by being lowered over the city wall in the middle of the night.

Saul in Jerusalem:

His return trip to Jerusalem was very different than his trip to Damascus. There was no comfortable stop at the home where he had spent the night before his arrival at Damascus. Upon checking his secretary's list, he had found that the name of Ananias had been added that last night on the road. And there would be no welcome for him at the home of the other friend he had visited.

He was now an outcast, and for the first time in his life, he understood what it meant to be an outsider, a person who needed a friend with whom he could share this new and wonderful life he had begun.

Even his secretary had made it clear that he wanted no connection with this new sect and would seek new employment as soon as they reached Jerusalem. And Saul certainly knew he would no longer be welcomed among the leaders at the Temple.

He decided to contact the disciples who were the closest to Jesus as soon as possible since he had much to say to them, and even more to learn from them. He learned that Peter and James the brother of Jesus were in Jerusalem, but a meeting with them did not go as smoothly as he had wished. The Hellenist Jews who had loved Stephen were still very hostile to Saul. He understood this, but his experience had been so clear, so unmistakable, that he was frustrated by their doubts. He needed a friend; a friend who could speak for him, to convince them of his wish to join them in fellowship.

This was all too new for him, because he had never needed sincere friendship before. In the past, people had respected his position and had welcomed his patronage. But now, he learned that respect without sincerity was like bitter wine. Now he needed the sincerity that came with brotherly understanding; like that which he had found in Ananias of Damascus. In Jerusalem, he found only suspicious acceptance from Peter and James, no acceptance at all from their followers, and complete rejection from the Temple leadership.

The advice from all quarters was that he should leave Jerusalem. Peter's recommendation was to go back to Tarsus, his birthplace and his home as a young rabbi. There, he was much more likely to find acceptance of his new faith in Jesus, and with the passage of time, he might demonstrate the validity of his conversion.

Saul understood this banishment from the scene of his greatest persecutions, and so he returned to Tarsus to preach what he had previously condemned. He still considered himself a teaching rabbi, but now with a deeper, bigger message; a message of love rather than laws. It was slow at first, but his talent and his new conviction prevailed, and within a few years he found himself with a considerable following. Tarsus was a center of trade, and this together with his natural ability to speak with sincerity, resulted in a reputation as a powerful new preacher of The Way.

Saul is Called to Antioch in Syria: 45 AD

There were many cities named Antioch; at least four just in Syria alone. But the most famous of these was the Antioch on the Orontes River. It was a navigable waterway that opened onto the northeast corner of the Mediterranean, and made this particular Antioch so very well known.

Saul knew it as a place where The Way had taken root, so he was not surprised when a special request came from there. It came from a man named Barnabas, who, like Saul, worked as an evangelist. Barnabas was committed to this work, but soon found that he lacked the talent of persuasion needed in such a cosmopolitan city.[28] The specific request was for Saul to join Barnabas as a preacher in Antioch.

Barnabas had never intended to be an evangelist. Born into a wealthy Jewish family on the island of Cyprus, he had lived a life of generosity and caring for the poor until he had been attracted to Jerusalem to learn and live as an orthodox Jew. He had gained favor at the temple and had been sent to Antioch as an investigator into reports of heresy perpetrated by members of The Way.[29]

The population there was large and quite international; Syrians, Jews, Greeks, and Romans. They favored innovative lifestyles and new ideas. There were so many new ideas that people were often "tagged" with a name that reflected their association. Followers of Cicero were called Ciceronians. Followers of The Way, who claimed a Jewish "Messiah", or as the Greeks said it, a Jewish "Christ", became known as "Christians".

Barnabas had come to Antioch as a Jewish investigator, sent by the Temple at Jerusalem to deal with

---

[28] Acts 11: 26
[29] Acts 11: 22

this Christian heresy. However, he soon found that he agreed more with the heretics than with the leaders in Jerusalem. What he had come to subdue, he stayed to preach. But his ability to preach well failed him.

That's when he heard of the Christian evangelist in Tarsus named Saul; the same Saul whom Barnabas remembered as the eloquent, but misdirected, prosecutor when Stephen had been killed by the Sanhedrin. He decided he could have no better helper in Antioch than that same prosecutor; Saul now renewed in Christ.

Famine and Dispute at Jerusalem: 46 AD

So Saul joined Barnabas in Antioch, and they preached of Christ's love for all humanity for a year together in Antioch. The church grew in numbers and prosperity. But recent crop failures and lost harvests had left Jerusalem in want. Because of this, the church at Antioch undertook to supply what they could for the relief of Jerusalem. Barnabas and Saul were chosen to take these gifts, along with their congregation's respect to their friends in Jerusalem.

To assist them, a Gentile convert to Christianity named Titus, went with them. Being uncircumcised, he represented a new factor in the process by which Gentiles joined this offshoot of the Jewish faith. Saul had accepted him as a full member of the congregation in Antioch, which was now referred to as Christian. This acceptance had been solely on his confession of faith in Jesus as the

Christ; the Messiah; the incarnate God. This agreed with Christ's teaching that He had come to fulfill the law; to pay the huge, but just, penalty for the all the sins of the world. His sacrificial death on the cross had paid the penalty. No sacrifice, penance, or bodily scar could add an iota to the Crucifixion of Jesus. No penance designed by Moses or High Priest was needed. The price was too high. Only God could pay it. And it was finished.

All three, Barnabas, Titus, and particularly Saul, knew that the acceptance of Titus on faith alone would cause a serious problem in Jerusalem. But they hoped that coming as benefactors to the needs of their fellow Christians would help to resolve the dispute they knew would come on the matter of required circumcision.

This new policy for acceptance, which would become known as the Antioch Innovation, would be difficult for Jews who had already suffered circumcision. They might well take the position that one must first be a Jew in order to become a Christian. And this would require circumcision.

Indeed, this was the case. A conference was held in which thanks were rendered for the material support from Antioch, but the innovation in the requirement for membership was severely disputed. Some, who saw no possibility of reconciliation, gave up the attempt and reverted to traditional Jewry. But Peter, James, and John ultimately agreed to Saul's policy of acceptance upon only the open declaration of faith.

In recognition that many new converts would come directly from a traditional Jewish background the decision was made that Peter would evangelize primarily to the Jews who would prefer to undergo the traditional rites, and Saul could witness primarily to the Gentiles among the Greeks in the Hellenist synagogues.

The reconciliation of this dispute was followed by a period in which Saul was active in the distribution of food brought from Antioch and was slowly repaid with forgiveness for his past as a persecutor. His return from Damascus, almost ten years previously, had been a terrible disappointment for him, in which he had been doubted and rejected. But his love for Israel, his land and his people had never faded.[30] He now found himself honored, and at home in the holy city.

He remained in Jerusalem for the following winter, encouraged and hoping to remain there permanently. He was now accepted as a teacher and advisor, but he was troubled by suggestions that he should leave the city to witness to foreign Gentiles. But that seemed contrary to the evidence before him. He was now reconciled to his people, and he wanted to stay there in Jerusalem. However, he was not certain as to what God wanted.

So he went to the Temple to pray, in the hope for guidance that would allow him to stay in Jerusalem. But God spoke to him with a clear instruction.

---

[30] Rom. 9: 1-5

"Depart; for I will send you far away to the Gentiles".[31]

God again had a plan that was different from his own. He came to understand that he should serve as a missionary to foreign lands, to people who knew nothing of Jewish history, customs, or religion. His would be a broad and more dangerous vineyard.

Ordination at Antioch: 47 AD

Barnabas agreed to go with him on this adventure, but they agreed that they would need a younger man, an apprentice, to carry out the lesser but essential tasks of any mission. Fortunately, Barnabas had an appropriate young relative named John Mark, whose home was in Jerusalem.

Since Saul's greatest evangelical success had been among the Gentiles of Antioch, and the food mission to Jerusalem had been on their behalf, it was decided to request ordination from that church. This would be a first experience for this congregation. As yet, they had no elders to officiate, but there were some who were good teachers. So Antioch agreed to sponsor this mission that would tell the world of the Christian way.

---

[31] Acts 22: 21

PART III - Paul

Saul Becomes Paul:

He was now convinced that his talent and his destiny were to serve God by carrying the good news that the Messiah had come, incarnate, in the person of Jesus. They would go first to the synagogues of the Jews as a starting point, and then to the Gentiles.

Now he preached what he had condemned. His new friends had been his old enemies, and his old enemies were now his friends. Strangely, his newfound fear was of his old friends, since they were the ones who had killed John, Jesus, and Stephen. And now he wept bitterly at the thought of those years.

He was a new man now. A man reborn on the road to Damascus and dedicated to the greatest transformation the world had yet experienced. He would now travel and live in lands where Jews would be the minority, and his Roman citizenship, inherited from his father, could be his greatest asset. For all of these reasons, but primarily to establish his new identity, he decided to use his second name; his Greek name, Paul.

As a first destination, Barnabas suggested that Cyprus, his own birthplace, would provide a perfect place to begin. There were some Jews there, and he knew friends who could help them if needed. So with John Mark as their helper, all three went to Antioch's port city,

Seleucia. by the Sea. There, they could find a ship to carry them to Salamis on the eastern coast of the island. Cyprus would serve as a good place to acquaint themselves with the problems of traveling lightly and dealing with the difficulties inherent to the life of defenseless missionaries.

Paul and Barnabas would depend exclusively on John Mark[32] to deal with most of the details concerning their food and travel arrangements, while they focused on their positions as teachers and spiritual advisors.

A major part of Mark's job was in making the travel plans even though he was not well acquainted with the geography of the region. In fact, most ship masters were only roughly aware of the few available charts and navigational skills were learned from experience or the advice of other sailors.

Barnabas had informed Mark that Paul's plans went far beyond Cyprus, to the southern coast of present day Turkey. From there, the plan was to travel by land, going eastward along the Mediterranean coastline. This would take them back to Tarsus for a period of rest before returning home to Antioch.

Thankfully, the crossing to Salamis was a short one with many ships making the passage. This meant that

---

[32] Most historians believe this John Mark was the same Mark who wrote the Gospel of Mark. Therefore he will be referred to henceforth simply as Mark.

Mark could begin this aspect of his duties with an easy selection from among several suitable ships.

They had expected that their arrival at Salamis would provide a propitious beginning; but it failed to do so. Paul's plan had been to speak only at whichever one of the local synagogues had the largest attendance. However, it was necessary to visit all of them since he was considered to be only a repentant persecutor of the Christians to whom he now owed apologies. The result was that they gave him suspicious understanding, but no acceptance of what he preached.

Their plan had been to pass quickly through Cyprus, traveling to Paphos on its west coast, and then by sea to a port on the western end of Cilicia. They had expected the island would be an easy journey since other Christians had preceded them, and Barnabas was well-known as a native of the island.

However, the reality was quite different. Their progress was slow and without success. Their travel pattern widened, first going north, and then turning south in repeated deviations from their general direction of westward toward Paphos. The only consistency lay in their repeated failure to win acceptance of their message.

It was not until their arrival in Paphos that their efforts did achieve a very special form of success. The entire island of Cyprus was ruled by a Roman Proconsul named Sergius Paulus. Paul may have considered it helpful that he and the Proconsul had similar names, but there was also another factor. Under the theory that "my enemy's enemy is my friend," the Proconsul might consider it wise to become friendly with these Christians. Friendship to Christians could become a political card he could play against Jerusalem.

However, Sergius prided himself as an educated man who looked to various sources for guidance. Among his advisors, he included an astrologer named Elymas. Having already heard of this Christian mission, Sergius summoned Paul and Barnabas to a consultation along with his advisor Elymas. Paul welcomed this meeting because of the potential impact it could have, not only within Cyprus but for his upcoming travels in Roman Cilicia.

In compliance with the wish of the Proconsul, this astrologer remained silent during Paul's exposition of the gospel, preferring to first hear what this new religious idea offered. All went well until Elymas realized that his lucrative position would come under threat, and he began interrupting and trying to twist Paul's words into contrary meanings.

Eventually, Paul became so angry that he spoke bluntly. He accused Elymas of being wickedly deceptive. The astrologer was unable to defend his position and lost the confidence of Sergius Paulus. Paul's argument proved far more reasonable to the Proconsul, and Sergius Paulus was converted to Christianity; a tremendous step forward for Paul and Barnabus.

Paphos to Perga: Late June, 47 AD

Encouraged by the success with the Roman governor on Cyprus, Paul's mission now sailed to the mouth of the Cestrus river, which lay at the western end of the Roman Province of Pamphylia. It was a small province, stretched along the Mediterranean coastline of what is now Turkey, and provided the most direct passage eastward to Tarsus and Antioch in Syria.

They traveled six miles up the Cestrus to the city of Perga, which was the intended starting point for this part of their mission. It was expected to offer great success because there had been no previous Christian efforts along this coast, and therefore no hostility toward Paul because of his history as a persecutor. However, the plan of successful progress along this coastline sadly came under question.

It was now July, the hottest season of the year, and traveling the coastal region would be a humid, semi tropical journey through an area infested with malaria. Paul was already suffering headaches and fever, probably symptoms of an earlier exposure to malaria. He therefore proposed to change direction and go northward, up into the cool, dry mountains of Pisidia.

However, this change in plan would involve some danger. It meant a climb of 4,000 feet into the mountains of central Turkey, where they knew of a synagogue in the city of Pisidia Antioch. It would be a dangerous climb over a twisting, turning trail on which they might encounter bandits. These were ex-pirates who had been driven inland under the pressure of Roman law enforcement along the coast.

At this point, their young helper, Mark, made a serious objection to this change from the original plan. Barnabas agreed with Paul to the change, but Mark was so serious in his objection that he returned to Jerusalem.

This change in plan introduced yet another problem. A return to Tarsus from Pisidia Antioch would require a prolonged journey over the Taurus Mountains to the east. However, Paul was persuaded not only because of his health, but because he wanted the chance to plant Christian churches along the key inland routes which connected Europe to Asia-minor.

History would record Paul's choice as a wise one, both for his health and his mission. He was saved from further exposure to malaria which proved to be a lifelong ailment for him, and this climb to Antioch in the mountains became extended through three additional cities. This provided a chain of Christianity from west to east through the highlands of what is now Turkey.

Upon reaching this Antioch in the Pisidian region, Paul and Barnabas took two weeks to recuperate and become familiar with the city. Then they went to the synagogue, intending to preach the resurrection, knowing that there would be "God Fearers" present in this synagogue. These were Gentiles who believed in the one God of the Jews, but did not commit to the rites of Judaism.

After honoring the usual ceremonies, the leaders of the congregation asked Paul to speak. "So Paul stood up, and motioning with his hand he said: 'Men of Israel, and you that fear God, listen.' "[33]

This simple opening was deceptively significant. As all who were present knew, it was the custom that a teacher of Judaism should speak while seated. And with his opening sentence, he also used the rhetorical style of the Greeks, using one's hand to express an attitude. These things showed his message was intended not just for the Jew, but for the uncircumcised God Fearers as well.

He then spoke to all present as "Brethren, sons of the family of Abraham, and those among you that fear God; to us has been sent the message of this salvation."[34] This made clear his fundamental belief that while Christianity came first to the Jew, it also included the Gentiles. His mission was to the Jew and the non-Jew; that is to say, everyone.

---

[33] Acts 13: 16
[34] Acts 13: 26

He then proceeded with a complete exposition, beginning with John the Baptist and ending with the death and resurrection of Jesus as the Son of God. This was revolutionary! This was not just a visiting rabbi. This was a rabbi who treated the Gentiles as part of the family of Abraham; and that the Messiah had come to all!

Among the amazed God Fearers was a man named Luke, a physician who had treated Paul's lingering symptoms of malaria when he had reached the city. [35] This was the same Luke who later recorded the account of this amazing sermon high in the mountains of Pisidia.

Thanked by those who believed but rudely rejected by many others, Paul left this city and continued on their way to the city of Iconium, a hundred miles eastward toward the Taurus Mountains in the east.

On to Iconium:

The road to Iconium was difficult, and their progress was very slow. This gave them ample time to critique each other's performance at Pisidia Antioch, their first effort in this new and formidable land. They had two donkeys; one to carry their impedimenta, and another for a rider while his fellow missionary walked alongside. In addition to saving the expense and annoyance of a third stubborn beast, this facilitated conversation which was often inspired by the scenic views along the way.

---

[35] See Smith; *Life and Letters*, Appendix iv

During one long stretch of remarkable but already discussed scenery, Paul reviewed his spotty record of success. This was very typical of him, seeing their performance as "his". First, because he was reluctant to attribute any fault to Barnabas; and second, because Paul was the heart of the mission. He had a unique ability to bring together voice, hands, and countenance of face that made listeners happy to have been enlightened by him. He had an inspired talent for speaking.

He loved Barnabas, who had willingly assumed the tasks vacated by the departure of Mark. He also needed Baranabas as a sounding board and as an honest critic. His opinions were always helpful on the many decisions they faced. But Paul knew that success or failure would be his alone. And so far, it had been a mixed success. They had succeeded with the Proconsul of Cyprus, and with a few of the leaders at Pisidia Antioch as well. But why not the others? Could it be that God intended just a few limited successes highlighted against a broad background of failures?

Suddenly, his donkey jolted him unexpectedly. There was no real concern about falling; it was merely the result of placing its hoof on a loose stone. But Paul smiled, thinking the beast would soon learn the benefit of proper hoof placement.

Then he saw a graceful connection to his own "failures". He recalled a lesson learned while training to be a tentmaker; the benefit of learning by doing. Maybe he'd become a better missionary simply by conducting more missions.

Those believers left behind at the synagogue in the mountains would certainly become better Christians as they witnessed to their doubting friends. But just as certainly, they would have failures. And they would learn from those failures, just as he had learned to become a better tent maker.

This excited Paul and he saw the need for yet another change in his plans. That synagogue at Pisidia Antioch was just a foundling! A new church that required nurture just as a babe needs milk.

Instead of going all the way through the Taurus Mountains to Tarsus, he should continue as far east as practical, and then turn back. Go back to revisit the churches he had just planted. Go back to strengthen their young sinews. This would also give him the experience he needed to help young churches that needed his advice and encouragement!

His preference had always been to witness first to the Jew and then to the non-Jew. But now he saw a need to carry this further. As these congregations grew in Christianity, he must foster their growth through re-visitations and writing letters. This would allow him to serve as a mentor. His mission will now go first to the Jew, then to the Gentile, then back to the new Christian.

Iconium and Lystra:

This region had been favored since the time of Caesar Augustus with a Roman highway called the Royal Road. It was well drained and smooth between Antioch and Lystra, a city which lay southwest of Iconium; their immediate destination. This road, like all Roman construction, was very well done and provided the best way to travel for most of the way to Iconium. But all too soon, they had to leave it for a less traveled road to reach Iconium. By leaving the Royal Road, they left behind more than just good road construction. There were no Roman outposts near Iconium, which meant leaving Roman law and order behind them.

There was a synagogue in Iconium, but word of Paul's stay in Antioch had preceded him and his welcome to Iconium was not as warm as he had hoped. The leaders at the synagogue were tolerant at first, but they soon asked the missionaries to take their message elsewhere.

Ironically, this rejection by the Jews produced some interest among the Gentiles in the region. At this, the Jews lost all patience and argued loudly against Paul. The result was that he decided to witness instead to the people who lived on the outskirts of Iconium.

But even this was thwarted because the people in the countryside spoke only a local dialect and did not understand the common Greek. This made it even easier for Paul's opponents to incite attacks against him and his mission. With no help from the Jewish officials, and no law establishment to protect them, Paul and Barnabas chose to move on to their next destination, Lystra.

This was a distance of about thirty-five miles to the southwest, over a road that was just as bad as the one which had taken them into Iconium. And yet, hoping to shake the dust of that city from their robes, Paul and Barnabas made the trip in one long day of travel.

Lystra boasted a Roman outpost which served as the eastern terminus of the Royal Road, and a population more respectful to travelers. There was no Jewish community in Lystra and no synagogue, so their message was directed to people who knew nothing of the wondrous prophecies that were fulfilled in Jesus as the Messiah.

There was, however, a Jewish family which contributed to the success of their mission. A widowed Jewish mother named Eunice had a son called Timothy, who was uncircumcised because his father had been a Gentile. Paul and Barnabas were welcomed by this small family and lodged with them for their entire stay in Lystra. Paul found that Timothy had been faithfully taught in Judaism, and he would serve as a friend and companion when Paul later returned to Lystra on a subsequent missionary journey.

There then occurred an incident worthy of special note. While preaching in the marketplace, Paul noticed a crippled man who seemed to be intent on understanding the message. Paul noticed this, and felt a sudden conviction to attempt a miraculous healing. He approached the man and said to him, "Stand upright on your feet."[36] The man immediately rose and walked, exciting all who witnessed it since they had never seen anything like this.

The people then shouted in their own local language, which was not understandable to either Paul or Barnabas. In their excitement at this wonder, the people celebrated Paul and took him and Barnabas to the Temple of Zeus, where their priest instituted a sacrificial ceremony to honor these strangers, who they now considered as gods.

When Paul and Barnabas saw what was happening, they tore their garments to condemn such heresy. The people were aggrieved at this rejection of their heathen beliefs, and were further incited by a group of Jews who had come from Pisidia Antioch. Then, encouraged by his enemies, the people of Lystra attacked Paul with stones.[37] He was knocked unconscious, and as he lay unmoving they were satisfied that they had killed him.

The presence of the Roman outpost caused the perpetrators to fear the consequences of such lawless behavior, so they dragged his body outside the city and left it there. When his friends heard of this, they found

---

[36] Acts 4: 8-10
[37] 2 Cor. 11: 25

him and revived him. He was then taken to his lodging in the Jewish home of Eunice and Timothy to recuperate.

Paul and Barnabas were amazed by this turn of events in Lystra. First worshiped as gods, then stoned as enemies. They had done all that could be expected in Lystra and agreed to move on to Derbe, the final point in their efforts to penetrate this region.

Peaceful Derbe:

Derbe was the sort of small town where a tired missionary would long to be. It was small; a place where little happened but where people knew everyone else and travelers were welcomed as a novelty. Paul and Barnabas were appreciated as a welcome contact with the outer world, bringing news of great things.

Percentage-wise, Derbe produced far greater success to their evangelism than the earlier stops on their long journey. One of their successes was a simple man who is still remembered in scripture as Gaius of Derbe.[38] He is still remembered for the help he provided for two tired missionaries 2,000 years ago.

The End of the First Journey: Winter, 48 AD

Now Paul began his plan to revisit every one of the Christian conclaves they had created on this, the first of

---

[38] Acts 20: 4

three such journeys. After enjoying Derbe, where they had not been driven out because of their Christian beliefs, they turned back to face again those cities which held such mixed memories.

Lystra, where Paul had been stoned as Stephen had been; Iconium, where the Jewish leaders had railed against them; and Pisidia Antioch, where he had dared to include the "God Fearers" as recipients of God's grace.

At each place, teachers of the good news were encouraged and strengthened; elders were selected as spiritual guides; and advice was provided to answer the many questions posed by any new congregation. It was clear that such support would be required for years to come, until these seedling churches could send their own apostles throughout Galicia.

Upon reflection, Paul did not see this first journey not as a series of failures to his body nor to his cause. Despite the physical abuse he had suffered, he considered such pain as his joyful unity with that of Jesus. And the cause had prospered tremendously in that Cyprus and Galatia were now fields planted for a harvest that would last for millennia.

Upon nearing Perga, where they had changed direction to face the hardship of the mountains, their preference for an early departure took them to the busy port of Attaleia. There, they found a ship that would bypass Cyprus and make the long passage directly to Antioch in Syria, which they reached in June of 49 AD.

The Impact of the First Journey: Summer, 49 AD

This first missionary journey that Paul undertook to spread the good news had covered 1500 miles, with about 500 of that by sea. In modern terms, that is not a significant distance. And although they were arduous miles, they were not notable for mileage even in biblical times. However, Paul later made a 2nd and even a 3rd missionary journey, each of which covered a distance that was more than twice as long, taking the gospel deeper into the lands and culture of Europe.

But the great success of the 2nd and 3rd journeys, which were indeed significant, was predicated upon the establishment of a foundational principal that resulted directly from this first journey. This principal was established for all time at a conference in Jerusalem in 49 AD and involved all the leaders of early Christianity. This included Peter, Paul, and James the brother of Jesus.

A Fundamental Doctrine:

When Paul and Barnabas arrived home at Antioch in Syria, they had unwittingly run into a hornet's nest. Jews from Pisidia Antioch had already arrived for the Passover festival in the spring of 49 AD and had made it known that Paul was accepting into church fellowship mere "God Fearers" and other Gentiles who had not submitted to the Mosaic laws.

These laws were of paramount importance to most Jews. They had been established more than a thousand years before by Moses, and served as the basis for their religious beliefs and cultural practices. Chief among these were circumcision and ritual cleansing.

What Paul was doing was not acceptable to the Christians who had been converted from Judaism. Paul and Barnabas had known this would be an important matter, but had assumed that it had been settled two years before, when it had been decided that Peter would witness to the Jews and Paul would deal primarily with the Gentiles. However, the Jewish Christians had apparently never intended that Gentiles could become Christians without first submitting to the laws of Moses.

Without an amicable resolution, there could be no dealings, commercial or social, between the Jewish Christians and the Gentile Christians. Jewish law and customs prohibited business dealings, and possibly even hospitality toward non-Jews; particularly to those who laid claim to the Jewish Bible. As things stood, Jews who accepted Jesus as their prophesied Messiah would have nothing to do with uncircumcised Christians. Yet this contradicted a basic Christian admonition to love one another. To be one church, a resolution was needed and it must be addressed before further mission journeys could begin.

The Council at Jerusalem: Autumn 49 AD

The needed resolution was made possible through the efforts of three men; Paul, Peter, and James. James reigned in Jerusalem and was recognized as the head of the disciples. As a result, all who were concerned met in Council at Jerusalem and prayed for a solution.

Much depended upon the temperament and wisdom of these three men. Paul was self assured and decisive. Peter was impetuous and yet inclined to protect the old ways. James had had doubts about his own brother at first, but came to recognize Him as Messiah. All three would play important roles in this council.

Peter began as a proponent of the conservative view that the old laws must be upheld, and that Christianity must be considered as a sect within Judaism. But Paul saw this as a perfunctory opinion. He was sure that Peter was simply trying to represent a faction that had to be represented in the dispute.

The real dispute was based upon the fact that the Jewish people were unquestionably the Chosen people of God; chosen to be the nation through whom God would reveal both His commandments and His love. They believed that the ancient covenant had made them His chosen people; that they belonged to God. But then, as time passed, they somehow came to believe that God belonged to them; that they had become the gatekeepers to God.

Peter readily saw the error in this reasoning, but his impetuous nature had led him to seek a quick resolution; one that avoided the difficult task of finding a theological solution. He had seen the problem the way a fisherman might see a break in his net. He preferred a quick solution; just tie the raw ends together. Better to have a working net, even if it still had a big knot in it. At least this would end all the troublesome debate.

The conservative view compelled compliance to the myriad of Jewish practices in order to worship the Lord who merely asked that we try to follow His Commandments while we love one another. But Paul vigorously challenged Peter, saying to him, "If you, though a Jew, live like a Gentile and not as a Jew, how can you compel the Gentiles to live like Jews?" [39]

Although he had not been present with Peter that night in the Garden of Gethsemane, Paul knew how the impetuous Peter had drawn a sword to protect Jesus, and how Jesus had then patiently healed the Temple Guard whom Peter had attacked.

In response, Peter was chastened and submissive as he recalled the healing grace of Jesus. Peter then spoke to the Council; "Brethren, you know that in the early days God made choice among you, that by my mouth the Gentiles should hear the word of the gospel and believe. And God who knows the heart bore witness to them,

---

[39] Gal. 2: 11 - 14

giving them the Holy Spirit just as he did to us; and he made no distinction between us and them, but cleansed their hearts by faith." [40]

Then he reminded his fellow Jews that none of them had ever been able to satisfy the laws of Moses. "Now therefore, why do you make trial of God by putting a yoke upon the neck of the disciples which neither our fathers nor we have been able to bear? But we believe that we shall be saved through the grace of the Lord Jesus, just as they will."[41]

The "yoke" of which Peter spoke was the 613 commandments to which the Jews tried to adhere; but they had all failed to do so. The saving "grace" of which he spoke was that of the Lord Jesus. This was Peter's assent to Paul's view that works alone could never secure salvation, but that it is granted by the grace of God.

James, the brother of Jesus, now hoped to mollify the Jews regarding social contact with Gentile Christians. He suggested that a letter be written to stipulate concessions on matters of purification. These included abstention from adultery and a prohibition against the eating of meat that had been offered as a sacrifice to idols, killed by strangulation, or not properly drained of blood. This letter, which was to be carried by Paul and Barnabas on their next mission to the western churches, said:

---

[40] Acts 15: 7 - 9 Refers back to God's grace to Gentiles in Acts: 10: 44 -45
[41] Acts 15: 10 - 11

"The brethren, both the apostles and the elders,
to the brethren who are of the Gentiles in
Antioch and Syria and Cili'cia, greeting.

"Since we have heard that some persons from us have troubled you with words, unsettling your minds, although we gave them no instructions, it has seemed good to us, having come to one accord, to choose men and send them to you with our beloved Barnabas and Paul, men who have risked their lives for the sake of our Lord Jesus Christ. We have therefore sent Judas and Silas, who themselves will tell you the same things by word of mouth. For it has seemed good to the Holy Spirit and to us to lay upon you no greater burden than these necessary things: that you abstain from what has been sacrificed to idols and from blood and from what is strangled and from unchastity. If you keep yourselves from these, you will do well. Farewell."[42]

The work of the Council at Jerusalem had now been completed. The primary criterion for acceptance as a Christian would be faith in Jesus as the Christ.

However, a minor problem now arose between Paul and Barnabas. Barnabas had hoped to take his young cousin, Mark, with them on their second missionary journey. However, there remained animosity

---

[42] Acts 15: 23 - 29

by Paul against Mark, who had deserted him at Perga on the first mission. There was sharp disagreement on this, and it was decided that Barnabas would take Mark with him on a separate mission to Cyprus, while Paul would take Silas, a leading member of the Christian community, with him on his second missionary journey.

The 2nd Missionary Journey of Paul: Fall, 49 AD

Paul's second journey was about twice as long, in both miles and time, as compared to his first journey. During this second journey, Paul would be placed in personal danger on three separate occasions.

This expedition had two objectives; first to strengthen and encourage the churches created during the first journey, and secondly to establish new churches. A third, unexpected achievement was the penetration of Christianity from Asia Minor into Europe.

Re-visitation to the Christians on Cyprus was left to Barnabas and his cousin Mark. Paul would re-visit the churches at Derbe, Lystra, Iconium, and Pisidia Antioch. However, this time he approached these cities from the east, going by sea from Antioch in Syria to the port of Mersin in southeastern Cilicia. From there, he and Silas traveled a hundred miles westward through the Taurus Mountains to reach Derbe. They then continued west to Lystra, where Paul had been stoned and left for dead on his previous journey; then on to Iconium and Pisidia Antioch.

Antioch - Derbe - Lystra - Iconium - Pisidia Antioch - Troas
Philippi - Apollonia - Amphipolis - Thessalonica - Beroea - Athens
Corinth - Cenchrea - Ephesus - Caesarea - Jerusalem - Antioch

Paul's courage was quite remarkable, going back to these places while knowing what might await him. But his reward was great. For in Lystra, he found a replacement for the youthful helper lost when Mark had left him on the first journey.

There, in Lystra, he was reunited with Timothy, an uncircumcised Christian who submitted to this ritual, performed by Paul in order to strengthen their witness to the Jews at Lystra. Timothy was then accepted as a member of Paul's team and he took part in what ultimately became the expedition into Greece.

From Pisidia Antioch they moved, or more descriptively, they wandered toward Mysia in the northwest, unsure what path God intended for them. Paul had even contemplated going further north toward Bithynia on the Black Sea. They were clearly at a point where a decision was needed. Now deep into the western part of modern day Turkey, both Silas and Timothy might well have wondered why Paul had bypassed so many cities where they knew that at least a few fellow Christians might have welcomed them.

This whole adventure was new to Silas and Timothy, so they simply accepted Paul's leadership. They knew that his decisions were not based on fear. That had been proven when he had gone back into Lystra. But Paul was now indecisive, perplexed between further evangelizing in Galacia, or daring to go further to the west, possibly even into Greece itself.

His health would argue against either choice. He was not a well man, and had been repeatedly plagued with severe headache and weakness. Ultimately, his decision was to follow the path that seemed to offer the least resistance. His health and the rugged mountains in the north argued against that direction, so he chose the gentler path, which flowed directly down to Troas on the Aegean Sea.

This turned out to be a fortuitous choice; for it was by bypassing Mysia and going to Troas that Paul was reunited with his friend Luke, the Macedonian physician who had treated him in Pisidia Antioch.[43]

It is likely that Luke, while administering to Paul's health, may have also provided encouragement to carry the mission across to Macedonia and into Greece. At Troas, Paul stood at the crossing of two great avenues of the ancient world. He could see the Dardanelles, less than twenty miles away, where the land avenue from northwest to southeast, connected Europe to Asia. Here, it crossed the water avenue from southwest to northeast, connecting the waters of the Mediterranean, Aegean, Marmara, and Black Seas.

Being a cultured and fearless man, Paul gazed longingly across the Aegean to Greece, and pondered upon the future of this mission. To go westward would mean uncharted territory for Christians and involve

---

[43] It is in Acts 16: 10 that Luke, the author of the book of Acts, first indicates his presence by changing his testimony from the use of the pronoun "them" to "us".

unknown dangers. And yet he had already adopted the Greek forms of rhetoric, and now he longed for the chance to witness at the very source of Greek culture.

Just 140 miles away lay Neapolis, the port city for Philippi, where just ninety years before, war had raged to avenge the assassination of Julius Caesar. It was also the city named for the father of Alexander the Great, the young man whose armies had conquered the ancient world as far as India.

These Grecian factors acted as a magnet upon Paul's thinking. Alexander had marched from west to east to expand the culture of Greece. Paul now decided to expand the grace of Christ by sailing from east to west.

Across the Aegean to Philippi: Spring, 50 AD

Happily, Troas was a port city where Paul, Silas, Timothy, and now Luke, easily found a cargo ship that could carry them first to the small island of Samothrace and then on to Neapolis; just seven miles from Philippi.

On the first Sunday after reaching Philippi, Paul performed the first Christian baptism in European history. This memorable ceremony was performed for a woman named Lydia, who traded in purple-dyed clothing. These were very costly goods because of the difficulty in extracting purple dye from the secretion of snails. She was, therefore, a wealthy woman and she invited Paul's entire group to share her home while in Philippi.

But not everything was that easy for them. Paul encountered an instance where his evangelical efforts ran afoul of a local business. While in the city, an enslaved girl who had a reputation as a soothsayer took advantage of Paul by following him and shouting divinations about him and his mission. Her purpose was simply to attract attention to herself. Annoyed at this, he turned and asked her to desist from such disrespectful behavior, and she agreeably stopped doing it.

But this angered the owner of the enslaved girl, who profited from her fortune-telling, and he went to the magistrates and claimed that Paul was interfering with his right to practice business, and that Paul was encouraging people into foreign practices. Basically, he claimed that Paul was creating a public nuisance.

And with no further justification, Paul and Silas were arrested and summarily beaten to discourage further disturbances. They were then thrown into jail and had their feet locked into stocks. But they were not downhearted, and they sang hymns that told of confidence in their faith. This assurance was especially noticed by the jailer and the other prisoners, who recognized it as unusual courage.

Late that night, a powerful earthquake shook the building so violently that the doors to all the cells were unhinged and even the foot-stocks were broken open. The jailer, upon seeing that the prisoners were now free to escape, immediately expected the forfeiture of his life as a penalty for allowing the prisoners to escape.

Panicked, he was about to kill himself, hoping at least to save his family from punishment. But Paul shouted, "Do not harm yourself for we are all here." Paul had even convinced the other prisoners not to escape, which would have caused terrible consequences for the jailer. [44]

The jailer was so impressed by Paul's confidence and integrity that he earnestly wanted to become more like Paul. After hearing the reason for such courage, the jailer asked Paul to baptism himself and his entire household into the faith that Paul had revealed to him.

Upon hearing of all this, the magistrates sent officers to set Paul and Silas free. However, Paul chose to not allow the rulers to hide their perfidy. Instead, he said, "They have beaten us publicly, un-condemned men, who are Roman citizens, and have thrown us into prison; and do they now cast us out secretly? No! Let them come themselves and take us out."[45]

The officials were now afraid, having dealt so poorly with Roman citizens, and they came to the jail,

---

[44] Acts 16: 27 - 34
[45] Acts 16: 35 - 39

apologized for their wrongdoing, and escorted Paul and Silas from the jail.

Having achieved the justice which he had demanded, this incident added greatly to Paul's record of success. He had made converts from every social level in Philippi; from a slave girl to the middle class jailer and even to Lydia, one of the wealthiest citizens of the city.

The Egnatian Way to Thessalonica:

What is now called highway A2 in modern Greece was known then as the Egnatian Way. It connected the Adriatic Sea which was on the west coast of Greece to the Aegean ports of Thessalonica and Neapolis on the east coast. The road's attraction to Paul was that it provided an effective way to deliver the gospel to many people who were going to many places.

When leaving Philippi, they had to backtrack to Neapolis, and then turn southwest toward Amphipolis and Apollonia to complete their hundred mile trip to Thessalonica, most of it along this ancient but busy thoroughfare.

It was impossible to know the welcome Paul's message might receive in any particular city, but one thing was certain. Because it was revolutionary, it would produce opposition.

Thessalonica's population was a mix of Jews, God Fearers, and a variety of people with other beliefs. When enough of these had become attracted to Paul's message of good news to all people, the Jews became jealous of his success, believing that Judaism should reap some of the benefit of conversions from among the non-Jews in Thessalonica.

This resulted in ill-feeling which degenerated into rabble rousing, and the usual indications that it was time to leave. However, the seeds that promised a new relationship with God had been sown, even as those who sowed the seeds were driven off by the rain.

Bound for Beroea:

The friends Paul made in Thessalonica encouraged and assisted him in his departure at night. He continued along the Egnatian Way to Beroea, forty miles to the west. What a difference forty miles can make! There, he found a warm welcome. The Jews of Beroea listened enthusiastically to his presentations and then, under his guidance, searched the scriptures with him to verify what he was teaching.

However, good news travels quickly and when some of the unfriendly Jews of Thessalonica heard of his success, they sent men to voice their ill-will and to cause trouble for Paul and his companions. Amidst this new dissention, his converts in Beroea advised Paul to depart. And once again, he agreed that a change was needed.

Since his arrival in Greece, he had been pilloried in Philippi, threatened in Thessalonica, and bundled out of Beroea in the middle of the night. Despite these disappointments, he was certain about the long-term impact of his efforts.

He longed to continue the approach which he had used in Beroea. He hungered for research of the scripture with people who were open to new ideas and willing to engage in respectful debate. That was the sort of teaching, searching for the truth, that he had known as a student at the feet of his rabbinical teacher, Gamaliel.

He concluded that best place to find the philosophical soil in which to plant the word would be Athens. There, he was sure he would find minds that were ready for ideas that can confound the wise and yet be understood by children.

Athens:

While Athens offered Paul the opportunity for learned debate, which suited his abilities, there was still a great need for witnessing in Beroea. So Silas and Timothy remained there while friendly converts escorted Paul on a 250 mile journey to Athens, where he would assess the situation and send for them as needed.

His first impression of Athens was exactly what he had expected. He was encouraged by the attention he received as a new-comer with new but well-developed ideas. He expressed them with clarity to listeners who found his ideas both new and startling. Philosophers, both epicurean and stoic, sought him out for discussions in the marketplace of ideas.

As a result, he soon detected a significant difference between debate in Jerusalem where he had been educated, and debate as practiced in Athens. In Jerusalem, debate was used to reach a conclusion upon which to act. In Athens, however, debate was merely an entertainment. The Athenian philosophers felt no need to reach a conclusion and they certainly had no intention of taking any action. In simple terms, they were typical philosophers.

The epicureans disavowed any spiritual life at all, and the stoics believed there was no personal connection between mankind and whatever gods might exist. Paul's disagreement on these points gained him an invitation to speak before the Areopagus, a court of about thirty Athenian judges who sat not only for certain serious crimes but also provided an opportunity for public discussion of the many religions represented by the profusion of gods worshiped in Athens.

A copy of Paul's presentation at this court is now displayed on a bronze plaque at the site of this ancient court. It reads, "Men of Athens, I perceive that in every way you are very religious. For as I passed along, and observed the objects of your worship, I found also an altar with this inscription, 'To an unknown god.' "What therefore you worship as unknown, this I proclaim to you. The God who made the world and everything in it, being Lord of heaven and earth, does not live in shrines made by man, nor is he served by human hands, as though he needed anything, since he himself gives to all men life and breath and everything. And he made from one every nation of men to live on all the face of the earth, having determined allotted periods and the boundaries of their habitation, that they should seek God, in the hope that they might feel after him and find him. Yet he is not far from each one of us, for 'In him we live and move and have our being'; as even some of your poets have said, 'For we are indeed his offspring.'

"Being then God's offspring, we ought not to think that the Deity is like gold, or silver, or stone, a representation by the art and imagination of man. The times of ignorance God overlooked, but now he commands all men everywhere to repent, because he has fixed a day on which he will judge the world in righteousness by a man whom he has appointed, and of this he has given assurance to all men by raising him from the dead."[46]

As expected in a university city, his sermon was mocked by some, honored by a few, but mostly considered as a fodder for future debate. So Paul sent word to Silas and Timothy to join him, not in Athens, but at Corinth, fifty miles to the northwest.

---

[46] Acts 17: 22 - 31

Corinth:

Because of its location, Corinth was a key city for Paul's purpose. It lay on a narrow neck of land which connected the two large land masses that make up Greece; as if the nation were cut in two. This and another fact of geography, made Corinth a very important city.

Cargo ships going from Europe to Palestine encountered very turbulent seas if they dared to sail around the southern tip of Greece. A far more practical route was to unload goods at Corinth and transport them overland a mere three miles to a port called Cenchreae, on the east coast of this narrow strip of land.

So Corinth allowed access to people who traveled the entire length of the Roman Empire, but it also had an accompanying drawback. It was a center of prostitution, along with the decadency which that engendered. Several Temples of Aphrodite were located both in and near the city. The result was that every night a thousand "sacred" prostitutes ranged a city rife with transients. Later, in a letter addressed to the church at Corinth, Paul referred to this depravity in the city.[47]

The population of Corinth was therefore an ever changing population of transients and prostitutes, both of which hungered for a new life. These were not the vacuous philosophers of Athens, which meant that Paul

---

[47] I Cor. 6: 9 - 10, and *Unlocking the Bible*, by David Pawson, page 583

and his little group faced a challenging opportunity to serve God over the next eighteen months; longer than in any other city in this mission to Greece.

It was in Corinth where Paul made a change in his evangelical strategy. Because of a lack of support, and even opposition by the local Jewish hierarchy, Paul voiced his frustration with them by declaring his intention to forgo his practice of "To the Jews first, and then the Gentiles." His efforts in Corinth were directed to the non-Jewish population exclusively.

When he left Corinth, he carried with him the names of people to whom he could send letters of encouragement, and also respond to the very practical questions faced by a young church finding its way.

Cenchreae and Homeward:

He sailed from Cenchreae aboard a ship carrying goods to Caesarea, a city on the Mediterranean coast just sixty miles north of Jerusalem. The ship would also make a brief stop at the Roman city of Ephesus on the southwestern corner of present day Turkey. The ship was a deep-draft, fully loaded vessel with a square sail on a single mast. Because of this rigging, it had very limited ability to sail into the wind.

While standing on its deck, thinking like a ship's captain, Paul smiled as he realized that he was becoming quite knowledgeable about cargo vessels and how to sail them.

Ephesus, Caesarea, and Jerusalem:

Ephesus was just a stop-over point along the way to Caesarea. However, he took some time to visit the city's synagogue and debate with the local Jews. Apparently, he had cooled off after his decision while in Corinth to avoid debates with Jewish leaders. He could not stay long, but he had been warmly welcomed, and he promised to return to them soon, "if God wills."[48] He later fulfilled this promise when he returned on a third missionary journey.

His trip home to Antioch would have been simpler had he sailed directly to Antioch from Greece, but while in Cenchreae, he had taken a solemn vow to thank God for his success in Corinth. It was to fulfill this vow that he planed a visit to the Temple in Jerusalem.

Home to Antioch: Late 51 AD

His return to Antioch, in the fall of 51 AD marked the completion of his second and longest, missionary journey. He had traveled 3,000 miles over the last two years and had visited over twenty cities.

He would subsequently conduct his third journey

---

[48] Acts 18: 19 - 21

which would last from about 52 to 55 AD. As always, its purpose would be to establish new Christian churches in Asia Minor and Europe, and to provide the teaching, encouragement, and advice needed by all of those young churches during the very early days of this new and revolutionary understanding of God.

PART IV - The Final Witness

Paul's Arrest: Spring, 57 AD

By 57 AD, Paul's third journey which went through southern Turkey and Greece, had now been completed. It had been a long journey; almost three years spent just in the Greek city of Ephesus alone. It is not surprising therefore, that two events which have connections to this city provide excellent examples of the main sources of opposition that Paul faced in his preaching. First, was the the adverse impact upon particular commercial activities; and second, the opposition of conservative Jews.

Simply put, Christianity is incompatible with a business that is antithetical to its teachings. This was shown most clearly in something that happened in Ephesus during his third journey.

Ephesus was the site of the famous Temple of Artemis, one of the Seven Wonders of the Ancient World,. It had been rebuilt several times over the centuries, but the one seen by Paul had existed prior to Antipater of Sidon who described it in the year 140 BC. It was a magnificent structure and even its predecessors had been a magnate for tourists and worshipers for hundreds of years.

In Paul's time, the manufacture and sale of souvenirs made in the form of artifacts that honored the Greek goddess Artemis, constituted an active and very profitable business. The best and most expensive of these items were made of silver.

Paul's preaching against idolatry, while not specifically criticizing these popular items, had resulted in decreased sales. As a result, the traders in silver had organized a riotous demonstration against Paul, hoping to silence his message of Christ as the one God. A blow to the pocketbooks of those who profited from an activity outside of Christian behavior had produced a riotous opposition.

However, Ephesus was a city occupied by Rome, and Rome disapproved of riotous behavior. Their concern was for Roman Peace, and peace was far easier to maintain than to reclaim. So, as often happened, Rome's insistence on law and order protected Paul. The city officials and the Roman soldiers restored the peace.

The other significant opposition to Paul's efforts was Conservative Judaism. An example which illustrates this also had a connection to Ephesus. It occurred in Jerusalem after his third journey had been completed and it involved a Greek follower of Paul named Trophimus, who was a man from Ephesus.

It happened during the Festival of Pentecost in Jerusalem, and there were many Jews who had come from cities where Paul had preached Christianity. It was well known that Trophimus was a Gentile, and not only a friend of Paul but shared his beliefs.

It was also true that Paul made frequent trips to the Temple, but this should not have been surprising, since Paul honored many of the ancient Jewish customs, particularly that of giving thanks for a safe return from his journeys. However, those who wished Paul harm incited a disturbance, claiming that Paul had heretically taken the Gentile Trophimus onto restricted Temple grounds.

This could lead to dire consequences since Temple law prohibited a Gentile from entering the Temple grounds beyond a designated point. The penalty for this offence was death. There were clear signs posted to this effect, and even the Romans saw it as a capital offense.

Without justification, the claim was made that Paul had taken Trophimus beyond the barrier and into the prohibited portion of the Temple grounds. It took little to bring a crowd to a riotous frenzy on this sensitive topic. Paul soon feared for his life. His protestations could not be heard over the shouts to kill him, and he may have even feared the fate of Stephen.

But once again the Pax Romana saved him. The Roman commander in Jerusalem, a Tribunus Militum which was two military grades above a Centurion, heard of the ongoing riot, and acted swiftly to end it. He ordered Centurions and a cohort of between three to four hundred soldiers to dash from their barracks located in the nearby Antonia Fortress at the northwest corner of the Temple Mount. Luckily, the enraged crowd had already dragged Paul out of the Temple grounds entirely. Otherwise, the soldiers might have been prevented from coming to his aid.

To put an end to the riot, the Tribune decided to arrest Paul for his own protection and he was bound in chains. The Tribune then tried to find out why the mob had attacked this man, but accusations came so fast and confusing that he ordered Paul to be taken into the Fortress until matters could be sorted out.

This certainly would have protected Paul from further beating, but as he was being carried by the soldiers to the steps that lead up into the Fortress, he shouted to the Tribune asking to speak with him.[49]

Paul had been speaking to the crowd in Hebrew, which the Tribune could not speak, so he asked if Paul spoke Greek. Paul then identified himself as an educated Jewish leader and asked to be allowed to speak to the crowd in Hebrew while standing there on the steps of the Roman Fortress. The people had now quieted down, and thinking that Paul might resolve this thing peacefully, the Tribune gestured to the soldiers to step back and allow the man to speak.

---

[49] Acts 21: 35 - 40

Paul began by asking for silence as he identified himself as one educated by the famous Rabbi Gamaliel. He then related his history as a persecutor of the Christians and even described his agreement to the stoning of Stephen. Hearing this, the people listened quietly. But when he told of his baptism and his commitment to convert Gentiles to Christ, they were incited to violence again.

Seeing that a renewal of the riot was immanent, the Tribune ordered Paul to be taken inside the Fortress to be scourged and questioned, thinking this would surely satisfy the crowd.

Once inside, he was bound with leather thongs to prepare him for whipping. It was then that Paul made it known to a Centurion that he was a Roman Citizen and that it was unlawful to scourge a Roman Citizen unless he had been convicted of a crime. When the Tribune was informed of this, he questioned Paul himself to determine that it was the truth. Then he immediately stopped the preparation for scourging.

The next morning, the Tribune took Paul before the High Priest and the Sanhedrin, hoping they could resolve this dispute, which was actually a religious matter and violated no Roman law. But it was soon apparent that his hope for a solution was far too optimistic. For as soon as Paul spoke his first sentence, the trouble began again.

Paul had begun by simply saying, "Brethren, I

have lived before God in all good conscience up to this day." The current High Priest Ananias, immediately commanded a temple guard to strike Paul in the mouth.[50]

This exchange was Paul's final break from Temple authority. Both Paul and Ananias had broken the religious laws of Israel. The die was finally cast. Paul had been purposeful in addressing the Sanhedrin as "Brethren"; this was putting himself on an equal footing with the court and it was quite presumptive. He would have known that this word was challenging.

But the High Priest's order to strike Paul in the face had also broken the law. Paul had been a member of the Sanhedrin and by striking him, Ananias had gone too far. There ensued an exchange of views which allowed an inherent disagreement within the Sanhedrin to come to the surface. Paul was a Pharisee, a Jew who believed in life after death, and he was well aware that the court was split between members who were Pharisees and others who were Sadducees, those who denied the existence of life after death.

Paul intended to use this single theological distinction to serve his purpose in this meeting of the Sanhedrin. This distinction divided the court into two segments that were irreconcilable. He believed in life after death, and the sufficiency of faith alone. This had been his message for well over a decade, and now he

---

[50] Acts 23: 1 - 2

wanted to bring these two matters before the entire Roman world. He wanted the world to face the principal matters of life after death and God's grace through faith in Jesus, and he wanted to preach this in Rome before Caesar himself! He did not want these matters swept under the rug in a Jewish court. Paul wanted to take it to Rome.

The result of his challenge was to divide the Sanhedrin, and they could not resolve it. Paul simply but loudly proclaimed that the real reason for him being on trial was that he believed in the resurrection. This gained the support of Pharisees and the inexorable opposition of the Sadducees. The resulting turmoil showed the house of Israel divided, with physical attacks upon Paul in the midst of a trial conducted by the Sanhedrin! The Tribune gave up on any solution here and took Paul back to the safety of the Fortress Antonia.

The Plot to Assassinate Paul:

Those Jews, who had merely despised Paul as a heretic, now hated him. They saw him as being protected by Romans, people who were more interested in the maintenance of law and order than in the destiny of men's souls. Romans, that cared nothing about the God of Abraham! If anything was to be done about Paul's heresy, the ultra conservative Jews decided they needed to do something; immediately. [51]

---

[51] Acts 23: 12 - 15

So a group of about forty of them, took an oath to neither eat nor drink until they had killed him. The next morning, they went to Ananias and revealed their plan to kill Paul.

"You therefore, along with the council, give notice now to the tribune to bring him down to you, as though you were going to determine his case more exactly. And we are ready to kill him before he comes near." [52]

Fortunately, Paul's nephew[53] learned of this plot, went to the Fortress and reported what he had learned to Tribune Claudius Lysias, and warned him not to be tricked by the Chief Priest and the Sanhedrin. Claudius cautioned the young man to tell no one else about all this. He then instructed two Centurions to prepare to move Paul that very night with a guard of four hundred soldiers and seventy cavalry to the highest level of Roman government in Judaea, which was located in Caesarea.

He then wrote a letter to Antonius Felix,[54] the Imperial Procurator of Judaea, to explain why Paul was being sent to him. It described the disturbance at the Temple, why Paul had been detained, and the death plot against him. Claudius also reported that he had instructed Paul's accusers to take their accusations to him as the highest authority in the province.

---

[52] Acts 23: 15
[53] Acts 23: 16 - 22 Paul's nephew saves Paul. See page 44.
[54] Acts 23: 26 - 30

That night at about nine o'clock, Paul was escorted out of Jerusalem by a huge protective guard, and taken forty miles to Antipatris, a small city along the coast about halfway to Caesarea. The following day, after a well-earned rest, the Centurions decided that the cavalry alone would be sufficient protection for the remaining distance, and the foot soldiers were allowed to return to Jerusalem at a much slower pace.

Upon reaching Caesarea, Paul was comfortably housed and told that he would be kept there until his accusers arrived. The Procurator, Antonius Felix, had governed Judaea for the last five years and prior to that he had served in Samaria. So he was very aware of the ongoing disputes amongst the Jews.

Paul's Trial before Antonius Felix:

It was five days before High Priest Ananias arrived in Caesarea, together with some of the Temple elders and an attorney named Tertullus, who would speak for them. It was his task to make the formal presentation before Felix, knowing that it could lead to a sentence of death. Despite the seriousness of the charge, his accusation was almost frivolous. He addressed Felix.

"Since through you we enjoy much peace, and since by your provision, most excellent Felix, reforms are introduced on behalf of this nation, in every way and everywhere, we accept this with all gratitude. But, to detain you no further, I beg you in your kindness to hear us briefly. For we have found this man a pestilent fellow, an agitator among all the Jews throughout the world, and a ringleader of the sect of the Nazarenes. He even tried to profane the temple, but we seized him. By examining him yourself you will learn from him about everything of which we accuse him." [55]

Five days of preparation, and this was their case. Felix ignored the flattery, and noted that the worst charge had been that Paul was a "pestilent fellow". The accuser had ended with the request that Paul should provide "everything of which we accuse him." They intended Paul to supply the evidence against himself!

In his response, Paul first described the purpose of his visit to the Temple, and then pointed out that his accusers had provided no evidence of wrongdoing. He had simply been in the Temple to offer alms and had brought no one with him.

He then declared that his accusers were those Jews whose only complaint was that he had preached the resurrection. "Or else let these men themselves say what wrongdoing they found when I stood before the council, except this one thing which I cried out while standing among them, 'With respect to the resurrection of the dead I am on trial before you this day.' "

---

[55] Acts 23: 2 - 8

Felix was already familiar with Paul's teaching regarding eternal life, but that had nothing to do with this trail. He saw the case as an internal dispute on Jewish theology, and that it posed no threat to Rome. Like Pontius Pilate before him, Felix saw his sole purpose in this case was to avoid unrest among the people.

He needed a way out of this mess, so he said that he would rule on the case only when the Tribune, Claudius Lysias, came to testify. In the meantime, Paul would be kept in Caesarea under house arrest, but in relative comfort, with no limitations on friends who might visit or provide for his needs. This meant Luke, his friend and physician, could visit without restrictions.

A few days later Felix and his wife Drusilla, who was a Jewess, came to Paul asking to speak to him about faith in Jesus as the Christ, and other things such as self-control, justice, and the future judgment faced by all men. They spoke often, and as time passed, it became clear that Tribune Lysias had no intention of appearing at this trial. Of course, his absence had the tacit approval of Felix, who apparently wanted the trial to continue indefinitely.

And Paul had no objection to this version of "arrest". He had comfortable quarters, good food, and the freedom to walk the streets of Caesarea and enjoy this lovely Roman city on the shore of the Mediterranean. He was, in effect, the house guest of the provincial governor. It allowed Paul something he craved; the chance to write.

He wanted to write letters to the churches of Cilicia and Greece, and to receive their emissaries who came seeking advice from him, being the foremost missionary of their faith.

A full two years passed under these conditions, at which time Felix's tenure as the Imperial Procurator of Judaea came to an abrupt and scandalous end. Ananias had been replaced as High Priest by a man named Jonathan, with whom Felix was having problems. Felix resolved their disagreements by hiring assassins to murder the High Priest at a festival in 58 AD. This resulted in the replacement of Antonius Felix by Porcius Festus in 59 AD, and Paul's case was carried over as unresolved.

The new Procurator's first official act was to pay his respects to the Jews in Jerusalem. This was not done out of fear of the Jews of course, but as always, diplomacy was less expensive than constant irritations. While the new governor was in Jerusalem, the Jews took every opportunity to complain about the ongoing two-year-old trial in Caesarea. Their disingenuous suggestion was to have Paul brought back to Jerusalem for trial. But this was sure to end, not in a trial but an assassination somewhere along the way.

Festus understood all this, but also felt that this entire problem could have been avoided if Pontius Pilate had stood up to the Jewish leadership in the earlier case of Jesus. The new Procurator resolved not to repeat

Pilate's mistake, but to administer Roman law rather than Jewish revenge.

Paul's Trial before Porcius Festus:

After a week of making appropriate social contacts in Jerusalem, Festus reached Caesarea where he assumed his responsibilities as the newly appointed Imperial Procurator of Judaea. One of these responsibilities was to deal with the accusations against Paul. This was complicated in that, although he was embarrassed about Felix's killing of Jonathan, he also wanted to avoid being seen as giving in to Jewish revenge.

Several of Paul's accusers had accompanied Festus to Caesarea in order to resume the case under this new administration. There were the same old charges, and Paul again refuted them just as he had done before the Sanhedrin; saying that he was being persecuted because of his belief in the resurrection. Since this was a religious dispute between Jewish factions, Festus asked Paul if he would submit to an appearance before the Sanhedrin again, but this time in the presence of Porcius Festus himself. Paul appreciated this gesture, but knew he would probably never reach Jerusalem alive. So he refused, not wanting to die along a dusty Samarian roadway as the result of a carefully planned Jewish accident.

His official response was that his accusers had provided no evidence that he had broken any law of the Jews or of the Temple. Furthermore, he was a Roman citizen in a Roman court and had violated no Roman law. Why then should Roman soldiers be ordered to take him before a Jewish court?

As a Roman citizen, he knew that if his case could not be resolved by a provincial Roman court, then he could appeal for justice from the Emperor. So he made the ultimate appeal of a Roman; "I appeal to Caesar!"[56]

Paul's Trial before Agrippa:

Festus recognized this right of appeal to the Emperor, and he was willing to transport Paul to Rome for this purpose. But there was a problem. Such appeals required that the evidence which supported the accusations must accompany the accused. But there was no evidence. So the Procurator Festus made a last attempt to resolve the trial another way.

He offered to submit the matter to King Herod Agrippa II, in charge of the area just east of Caesarea. Agrippa happened to be the brother-in-law of the previous Roman Procurator, Antonius Felix, so he was already familiar with the case.

This offer was quite convenient for Agrippa and his wife Bernice, who was also his own sister. They were already in Caesarea to welcome the new Procurator to Judea.

---

[56] Acts 25: 8 - 11

Taking advantage of this perfunctory visit, Festus mentioned Paul's case to the King. Agrippa readily agreed since he already knew the details of the case and he looked forward to the notoriety he might achieve.

The next day, Agrippa and Bernice provided a touch of royalty to the proceedings. Festus had made sure that the leading families of Caesarea and his top military advisers were all present. He wanted to leave no stone unturned to assure that this would be the final episode of Paul's long stay in Caesarea. He opened the proceedings by addressing Agrippa.

"King Agrippa and all who are present with us, you see this man about whom the whole Jewish people petitioned me, both at Jerusalem and here, shouting that he ought not to live any longer. But I found that he had done nothing deserving death; and as he himself appealed to the emperor, I decided to send him. But I have nothing definite to write to my lord about him. Therefore, I have brought him before you, and, especially before you, King Agrippa, that, after we have examined him, I may have something to write. For it seems to me unreasonable, in sending a prisoner, not to indicate the charges against him."[57]

Paul, sure of his defense and having delivered it many times before, used the style of Greek oration with great skill in movement and rhetoric. He laid out his own

---

[57] Acts 25: 24 - 27

history as a well-meaning but cruel persecutor of Christians, his miraculous conversion, and then the vicious persecution he himself suffered during his missions of evangelization.

As he listened, Festus found nothing new in Paul's defense, and he became frustrated with Paul. So he got up and shouted at Paul, "Paul, you are mad; your great learning is turning you mad."

But Paul said, "I am not mad, most excellent Festus, but I am speaking the sober truth. For the King knows about these things, and to him I speak freely; for I am persuaded that none of these things has escaped his notice, for this was not done in a corner." [58]

Then the King and Bernice got up, together with the Procurator and those who were sitting with them. They all left the room to speak privately, and agreed that "This man is doing nothing to deserve death or imprisonment." And King Agrippa said to Festus, "This man could have been set free if he had not appealed to Caesar."[59]

---

[58] Acts 26: 24 - 26
[59] Acts 26: 30 - 32

Paul Goes to Rome: 59 AD

Despite the views of Procurator Festus and King Agrippa as to Paul's innocence, neither one of them had the courage to do anything about it which might have diverted the slow but inexorable flow of governmental bureaucracy. Paul would be taken to Rome.

Festus did not have any evidence to be sent to Rome, but he was still a competent politician. Surely he could have dictated a report composed of flattery, ambiguous opinions along with ineffectual suggestions, and yet say absolutely nothing. That might have sufficed. However, history remains silent as to what Festus did, or did not do, with regard to evidence transmitted to Rome.

Sailing from Caesarea to Rome was no easy task, particularly late in the year, when the winds were not favorable. There were three passengers; Paul, his faithful friend and physician Luke, and a Greek servant named Aristarchus. They would travel under the guardianship of a Roman Legionnaire named Julius. He was much more than just a jailer to prevent Paul's escape since Paul obviously had no intention of escape; he had demanded this trip.

Julius was a member of an elite unit, the Praetorian Guard. It was a cohort of soldiers, each of whom had a proven record of loyalty and bravery in combat. The unit had been formed eighty-six years previously by Caesar Augustus to serve as bodyguards for the Emperor, and other influential Roman officials. They were often involved in intelligence operations which, coupled with their innate military strength, actually made them a unique, but very real political force.

Just eighteen years previously, the Praetorian Guard had assassinated the Emperor Caligula and installed his own uncle, Claudius, as Emperor. This was because a group of courageous Senators had wanted to undue the work of Julius Caesar by returning Rome from an Empire back into a Republic, as it had been prior to the crossing of the Rubicon. Obviously the soldiers of the Guard owed their allegiance to either the Emperor, or whoever would be Emperor the next day; but certainly not to the people.

So Rome had remained an Empire, and during the past five years the Guard had been exerting a beneficial influence upon the current emperor, Nero. So it was to Nero to whom Paul now went to plead his case. Considering the influence exhibited by the Praetorian Guard, Julius might have been a better friend in Rome than either Festus or Agrippa.

The journey's first step was to find a ship, and as a provincial capital, Caesarea offered a good chance of finding a ship going directly to Rome. But this was not what they did. Instead, Julius selected a ship bound for Sidon, a short trip of just eighty miles north from Caesarea. This allowed Paul to visit friends whom he might never see again. In this, Julius showed himself to be a man of understanding and kindness.

Julius was the man in charge, and he could easily have found a ship that would have taken them much further and would have avoided this delay entirely. Instead, he allowed Paul to visit his friends. It was late in the sailing season, and the winds were from the west and growing worse every day.

Leaving Sidon, they made for the east coast of Cyprus, where they turned to the northeast in order to stay on the downwind side of the big island as they gradually moved northward to gain the southern shore of Cilicia. From there they sailed due west to the port of Myra, where they anchored in the harbor to recover after fifteen days of continual tacking into the west wind.

These cargo vessels were only slightly over one hundred feet long, with rigging that made it impossible to sail closely into the wind. It was even difficult for them to tack first left and then right, as they repeatedly inched windward.

While at Myra, Julius was fortunate enough to find a larger ship coming from Alexandria, which was bound directly to Italy with a cargo of Egyptian corn. So by the end of the third day they were off again into the wind, westward toward Cnidus, just a spit of land eighty miles straight south of Ephesus.

The basic plan had been to continue sailing westward from there; going straight across the Aegean. But this would have meant sailing straight into the wind and taking them indirectly into the dangerous waters at the southern tip of Greece.

Therefore, it was decided to change plans and sail from Cnidus toward the east end of Crete. There, they could get into the safer downwind side of that island, and then creep westward by hugging its southern shoreline. This provided protection from the wind until they anchored at the southernmost part of that island, a point appropriately called Fair Havens. Being only halfway along the length of Crete, it posed a difficult decision.

Despite its name, it was a very desolate beach and not a good place to take refuge. However, the nearest safe harbor was Phoenice, a harbor on Crete that lay about sixty miles of sailing westerly into the wind. They debated the choice to stay or to go, and Paul felt they should remain where they were. But this decision was influenced by a sudden change in the wind. It turned, coming from the south, which would allow them to reach the safety of Phoenice. So they weighed anchor to make the attempt.

Unfortunately, the west wind reasserted itself and their vessel went further out to sea, and the towed dingy became uncontrollable. When they came under the lee of an island called Cauda, twenty-five miles due south of Phoenice, they hauled it aboard to keep from losing it.

Realizing that they could no longer control the direction of the vessel, and that the heavy seas might break it into pieces, the crew passed very heavy ropes under the keel and over the gunnels in order to tighten them and thus hold the vessel together. They were now in a vicious storm, twenty-five miles out to sea, in a ship held together with ropes, and with no hope of reaching any harbor on the island of Crete.

The next day, they started throwing some deck equipment overboard in order to lower the vessel's center of gravity. On the third day, they jettisoned all of the ship's spare gear. After many more days of storm in which neither sun nor stars were seen, they had little idea where they were, and lost even the hope of survival.

It was some days later that the storm abated, and Paul offered them new hope. First, no one had eaten properly for many days, so he suggested they strengthen the body with food. Then he told them of a vision he had experienced. He had been told that he would stand before Caesar, and that all aboard this vessel would survive this voyage. They should renew their hope and that none would be lost.

Finally, in the middle of the night, after fourteen days of drifting across the Adriatic Sea, some sailors thought they had seen land. Soundings were taken and showed a depth of only 120 feet of water beneath them, which promised an approach to land. To prevent crashing into rocks during the night, four anchors were dropped from the stern.

Then some sailors put the dingy back into the water, saying they wanted to put anchors off the bow as well. But Paul suspected they were actually planning to desert the ship. He spoke to Julius the Legionnaire, advising that no one should leave the ship until morning lest a panic ensue. So soldiers were ordered to cut the lines to the dingy so that all those aboard would remain together as a united group.

In the morning, a beach was sighted and Paul suggested that they all eat to strengthen themselves for the task of reaching shore. After giving thanks to God for their deliverance, they began lightening the ship by casting the cargo of corn overboard. When sufficiently lightened, they headed the ship toward the beach until the bow struck. It held fast, but the surf then hit the stern and the ship began to break up.

There were other prisoners on board, and in the excitement, some soldiers feared the penalty of allowing prisoners to escape and thought they should kill the prisoners. Paul intervened and told those who could swim to leap into the sea and swim for shore. He told the others to hold wooden planks from the ship and make for the beach. Amazingly, all 276 on board reached shore safely. An amazing conclusion to a journey which wind and sea had fought and the very stars had hidden their guidance.

Safe on the Island of Malta:

They had now completed a six hundred mile voyage from Crete to Malta, which is the name of the island where their ship lay in tatters. But they were safe, and welcomed not only by the islanders but by Publius, the Chief of the island. His estate was nearby, and his hospitality was extended to Paul and his party for three days, even though Paul was still a prisoner.

Publius' father of was ill in bed at the time, and diagnosed by Luke as suffering from dysentery with intermittent fever. Paul went to the man's beside and prayed for his recovery. The father recovered, and this made a stir among the people who then came to be cured of various ailments. They also were cured, and it is likely that Luke, as a physician, served as the first Christian medical missionary.

Today, the beach on which they had landed is known as St. Paul's Island, at the northeast corner of Malta. There is a statue of Paul on a promontory of that island and the nearest town is called Saint Paul's Bay.

The remoteness of the island, the survivors' need for rest and recovery, and the hospitality of the islanders resulted in Paul staying there for three months. They then found a ship available to take them to Italy. The ship, named The Three Brothers, had arrived during the winter and now, on February 8, 60 AD, faithful Julius resumed his mission to escort Paul and his party safely to Rome.

Sailing north from Malta, the winds forced them to spend three days in the anchorage at Syracuse on the Island of Sicily. Then, while passing through the narrow Strait of Messina, the vessel was delayed for a day at the port of Rhegium.[60]

Then, with favorable winds from the south, they arrived at Puteoli on the north shore of the Bay of Naples. They were now just 140 miles from Rome. However, they stayed there several days since Julius needed to report his arrival and get further instructions and Paul needed a rest. He was tired and nervous. Having gone through the perils of the voyage, he now faced a stressful trial before the Emperor Nero.

He was escorted from Puteoli to the Appii Forum, an inn along the Appian Way where, just forty-three miles from Rome, he met Christians who came out to welcome him. The next day, a second contingent met him at the Three Taverns, another stopping point along the Appian Way; just thirty miles from the capital of the Empire.

These two greetings by fellow Christians were a joy to his spirits, and he now felt assured of what lay before him in Rome. There, he was given permission to live in his own rented house but in company with his Praetorian Guard, Julius. Within a few days, he had contacted leaders of the Jewish community to come and

---

[60] Life and Letters of St. Paul, David Smith, page 500

speak with him. He was well known to them of course, and so they came with varied opinions. Still, they wanted to meet him and listen with as much courtesy as possible.

These meetings were intended to give Paul a chance to present his message, as he had done so many times before to other Jews, and in so many other places. As usual, there were mixed reactions among them. Some were unchanged, some were intrigued, others believed. This was nothing new to him. It had been the case during all his years of offering Christ to all who would listen.

He said to the Jews in Rome speaking from Isaiah,

"You shall indeed hear but never understand,
and you shall indeed see, but never perceive.
For this people's heart has grown dull,
and their ears are heavy of hearing,
and their eyes they have closed;
lest they should perceive with their eyes,
and hear with their ears,
and understand with their heart,
and turn for me to heal them."

"And he lived there two whole years at his own expense, and welcomed all who came to him, preaching the kingdom of God and teaching about the Lord Jesus Christ quite openly and unhindered." [61]

---

[61] Acts 28: 26 - 31

The End and the Beginning:

There are various ideas on when, where, and even how Paul died. But all of that is of little consequence. What really matters is what he did, and there is much evidence on that. He lived a life that spanned about sixty-five years, was greatly loved and respected by some, and yet imprisoned and scourged by others. He was honored first in the loneliest outpost of the Roman Empire, and eventually even in its famous Capital. He had hated the faith which he came to love, and he had stoned a loving servant of the same God for whom he submitted himself to be stoned.

He suffered the battles of early Christianity, and as a faithful servant he established the universality of its message. He was talented in speech, and human enough to be very wrong. He was blessed with great visions, and the courage to fulfill them.

The end of his life was the transfer point where his apostolic baton was grasped by thousands of evangelical Christians to carry forward the good news of Jesus; the living Christ, the God who chose to also live for a while as a man, and now waits to return.

Postscript

The years following Paul's enigmatic passing into history have spawned various legends and strange stories about his death. And there truly is a large gap in our knowledge of those years after his arrival in Rome. The wish to fill that gap is like the hope of early navigators to fill the unhappy blank spaces on their nautical charts. However, I see little need for last-minute coordinates. His course is clear to all who look, and his destination already won.

He reached Rome in 60 AD and died about six years later with significant evidence of at least three letters written from there. That period gives historians a significant opportunity for research into the clues and traditions scattered throughout those years. But it really adds little to the primacy of Luke's own personal account.

However, for those with a very justifiable interest in this period, a scholarly treatment is provided in *The Life and Letters of St. Paul* by Professor David Smith. He begins his treatment with *The Historical Problem,* on page 579 and completes his study of this topic with *The Apostle's Martyrdom,* on page 641. His work is thorough, enlightening, and stands as a premier source on the life of Saint Paul, the greatest Roman.

Made in the USA
Columbia, SC
23 November 2021